PNIN

Vladimir Nabokov

ANCHOR PRESS / DOUBLEDAY
GARDEN CITY, NEW YORK
1984

All of the characters in this book are fictitious,
and any resemblance to actual persons,
living or dead, is purely coincidental

Copyright © 1953, 1955, 1957 by Vladimir Nabokov
All Rights Reserved
Printed in the United States of America

Library of Congress Cataloging in Publication Data

Nabokov, Vladimir Vladimirovich, 1899–1977.
Pnin.

I. Title.
PS3527.A15P59   1984   813'.54   83-22437
ISBN 0-385-19116-2

PNIN

PNIN

Chapter One

1

The elderly passenger sitting on the north-window side
of that inexorably moving railway coach, next to an
empty seat and facing two empty ones, was none other
than Professor Timofey Pnin. Ideally bald, sun-tanned,
and clean-shaven, he began rather impressively with
that great brown dome of his, tortoise-shell glasses
(masking an infantile absence of eyebrows), apish
upper lip, thick neck, and strong-man torso in a tight-
ish tweed coat, but ended, somewhat disappointingly,
in a pair of spindly legs (now flanneled and crossed)
and frail-looking, almost feminine feet.

His sloppy socks were of scarlet wool with lilac

lozenges; his conservative black oxfords had cost him about as much as all the rest of his clothing (flamboyant goon tie included). Prior to the nineteen-forties, during the staid European era of his life, he had always worn long underwear, its terminals tucked into the tops of neat silk socks, which were clocked, soberly colored, and held up on his cotton-clad calves by garters. In those days, to reveal a glimpse of that white underwear by pulling up a trouser leg too high would have seemed to Pnin as indecent as showing himself to ladies minus collar and tie; for even when decayed Mme. Roux, the concierge of the squalid apartment house in the Sixteenth Arrondissement of Paris—where Pnin, after escaping from Leninized Russia and completing his college education in Prague, had spent fifteen years—happened to come up for the rent while he was without his *faux col*, prim Pnin would cover his front stud with a chaste hand. All this underwent a change in the heady atmosphere of the New World. Nowadays, at fifty-two, he was crazy about sun-bathing, wore sport shirts and slacks, and when crossing his legs would carefully, deliberately, brazenly display a tremendous stretch of bare shin. Thus he might have appeared to a fellow passenger; but except for a soldier asleep at one end and two women absorbed in a baby at the other, Pnin had the coach to himself.

Now a secret must be imparted. Professor Pnin was on the wrong train. He was unaware of it, and so was the conductor, already threading his way through the train to Pnin's coach. As a matter of fact, Pnin at the moment felt very well satisfied with himself. When inviting him to deliver a Friday-evening lecture at Cremona—some two hundred versts west of Waindell,

Pnin's academic perch since 1945—the vice-president of the Cremona Women's Club, a Miss Judith Clyde, had advised our friend that the most convenient train left Waindell at 1:52 P.M., reaching Cremona at 4:17; but Pnin—who, like so many Russians, was inordinately fond of everything in the line of timetables, maps, catalogues, collected them, helped himself freely to them with the bracing pleasure of getting something for nothing, and took especial pride in puzzling out schedules for himself—had discovered, after some study, an inconspicuous reference mark against a still more convenient train (Lv. Waindell 2:19 P.M., Ar. Cremona 4:32 P.M.); the mark indicated that Fridays, and Fridays only, the two-nineteen stopped at Cremona on its way to a distant and much larger city, graced likewise with a mellow Italian name. Unfortunately for Pnin, his timetable was five years old and in part obsolete.

He taught Russian at Waindell College, a somewhat provincial institution characterized by an artificial lake in the middle of a landscaped campus, by ivied galleries connecting the various halls, by murals displaying recognizable members of the faculty in the act of passing on the torch of knowledge from Aristotle, Shakespeare, and Pasteur to a lot of monstrously built farm boys and farm girls, and by a huge, active, buoyantly thriving German Department which its Head, Dr. Hagen, smugly called (pronouncing every syllable very distinctly) "a university within a university."

In the Fall Semester of that particular year (1950), the enrollment in the Russian Language courses consisted of one student, plump and earnest Betty Bliss, in the Transitional Group, one, a mere name (Ivan Dub, who never materialized) in the Advanced, and

9

three in the flourishing Elementary: Josephine Malkin, whose grandparents had been born in Minsk; Charles McBeth, whose prodigious memory had already disposed of ten languages and was prepared to entomb ten more; and languid Eileen Lane, whom somebody had told that by the time one had mastered the Russian alphabet one could practically read "Anna Karamazov" in the original. As a teacher, Pnin was far from being able to compete with those stupendous Russian ladies, scattered all over academic America, who, without having had any formal training at all, manage somehow, by dint of intuition, loquacity, and a kind of maternal bounce, to infuse a magic knowledge of their difficult and beautiful tongue into a group of innocent-eyed students in an atmosphere of Mother Volga songs, red caviar, and tea; nor did Pnin, as a teacher, ever presume to approach the lofty halls of modern scientific linguistics, that ascetic fraternity of phonemes, that temple wherein earnest young people are taught not the language itself, but the method of teaching others to teach that method; which method, like a waterfall splashing from rock to rock, ceases to be a medium of rational navigation but perhaps in some fabulous future may become instrumental in evolving esoteric dialects—Basic Basque and so forth—spoken only by certain elaborate machines. No doubt Pnin's approach to his work was amateurish and lighthearted, depending as it did on exercises in a grammar brought out by the Head of a Slavic Department in a far greater college than Waindell—a venerable fraud whose Russian was a joke but who would generously lend his dignified name to the products of anonymous drudgery. Pnin, despite his many shortcomings, had about him a disarming, old-fashioned charm which Dr. Hagen, his staunch protector, insisted before morose trustees was a delicate imported article worth paying for in domestic cash. Whereas the degree in sociology and political economy that Pnin had obtained with some pomp at the University of Prague around 1925 had become by mid-century a doctorate in desuetude, he was not altogether miscast as a teacher of Russian. He was beloved not for any essential ability but for those unforgettable digressions of his, when he would remove his glasses to beam at the past while massaging the lenses of the present. Nostalgic excursions in broken English. Autobiographical tidbits. How Pnin came to the *Soedinyon-nïe Shtatï* (the United States). "Examination on ship before landing. Very well! 'Nothing to declare?' 'Nothing.' Very well! Then political questions. He asks: 'Are you anarchist?' I answer"—time out on the part of the narrator for a spell of cozy mute mirth—" 'First what do we understand under "Anarchism"? Anarchism practical, metaphysical, theoretical, mystical, abstractical, individual, social? When I was young,' I say, 'all this had for me signification.' So we had a very interesting discussion, in consequence of which I passed two whole weeks on Ellis Island"—abdomen beginning to heave; heaving; narrator convulsed.

But there were still better sessions in the way of humor. With an air of coy secrecy, benevolent Pnin, preparing the children for the marvelous treat he had once had himself, and already revealing, in an uncontrollable smile, an incomplete but formidable set of tawny teeth, would open a dilapidated Russian book at the elegant leatherette marker he had carefully placed there; he would open the book, whereupon as often as not a look of the utmost dismay would alter his plastic features; agape, feverishly, he would flip right and left through the volume, and minutes might pass before he found the right page—or satisfied himself that he had marked it correctly after all. Usually the passage of his choice would come from some old and naïve comedy of merchant-class habitus rigged up by Ostrovski almost a century ago, or from an equally ancient but even more dated piece of trivial Leskovian jollity dependent on verbal contortions. He delivered these stale goods with the rotund gusto of the classical Alexandrinka (a theater in Petersburg), rather than with the crisp simplicity of the Moscow Artists; but since to appreciate whatever fun those passages still retained one had to have not only a sound knowledge of the vernacular but also a good deal of literary insight, and since his poor little class had neither, the performer would be alone in enjoying the associative subtleties of his text. The heaving we have already noted in another connection would become here a veritable earthquake. Directing his memory, with all the lights on and all the masks of the mind a-miming, toward the days of his fervid and receptive youth (in a brilliant cosmos that seemed all the fresher for having been abolished by one blow of history), Pnin would get drunk on his private wines as he produced sample after sample of what his listeners politely surmised was Russian humor. Presently the fun would become too much for him; pear-shaped tears would trickle down his tanned cheeks. Not only his shocking teeth but also an astonishing amount of pink upper-gum tissue would suddenly pop out, as if a jack-in-the-box had been sprung, and his hand would fly to his mouth, while his big shoulders shook and rolled. And although the speech he smothered behind his dancing hand was now doubly unintelligible to the class, his complete surrender to his own merriment would prove irresistible. By the time he was helpless with it he would have his students in stitches, with abrupt barks of clockwork hilarity coming from Charles and a dazzling flow of unsuspected lovely laughter transfiguring Josephine, who was not pretty, while Eileen, who was, dissolved in a jelly of unbecoming giggles.

All of which does not alter the fact that Pnin was on the wrong train.

How should we diagnose his sad case? Pnin, it should be particularly stressed, was anything but the type of that good-natured German platitude of last century, *der zerstreute Professor*. On the contrary, he was perhaps too wary, too persistently on the lookout for diabolical pitfalls, too painfully on the alert lest his erratic surroundings (unpredictable America) inveigle him into some bit of preposterous oversight. It was the world that was absent-minded and it was Pnin whose business it was to set it straight. His life was a constant war with insensate objects that fell apart, or attacked him, or refused to function, or viciously got themselves lost as soon as they entered the sphere of his existence. He was inept with his hands to a rare degree; but because he could manufacture in a twinkle a one-note mouth organ out of a pea pod, make a flat pebble skip ten times on the surface of a pond, shadowgraph with his knuckles a rabbit (complete with blinking eye), and perform a number of other tame tricks that Russians have up their sleeves, he believed himself endowed with considerable manual and mechanical skill. On gadgets he doted with a kind of dazed, superstitious delight. Electric devices enchanted him. Plastics swept him off his feet. He had a deep admiration for the zipper. But the devoutly plugged-in clock would make nonsense of his mornings after a storm in the middle of the night had paralyzed the local power station. The frame of his spectacles would snap in mid-bridge, leaving him with two identical pieces, which he would vaguely attempt to unite, in the hope, perhaps, of some organic marvel of restoration coming to the rescue. The zipper a gentleman depends on most would come loose in his puzzled hand at some nightmare moment of haste and despair.

And he still did not know that he was on the wrong train.

A special danger area in Pnin's case was the English language. Except for such not very helpful odds and ends as "the rest is silence," "nevermore," "weekend," "who's who," and a few ordinary words like "eat," "street," "fountain pen," "gangster," "Charleston," "marginal utility," he had had no English at all at the time he left France for the States. Stubbornly he sat down to the task of learning the language of Fenimore Cooper, Edgar Poe, Edison, and thirty-one Presidents. In 1941, at the end of one year of study, he was proficient enough to use glibly terms like "wishful thinking" and "okey-dokey." By 1942 he was able to interrupt his narration with the phrase, "To make a long story short." By the time Truman entered his second term, Pnin could handle practically any topic; but otherwise progress seemed to have stopped despite all his efforts, and by 1950 his English was still full of flaws. That autumn he supplemented his Russian courses by delivering a weekly lecture in a so-called symposium ("Wingless Europe: A Survey of Contemporary Continental Culture") directed by Dr. Hagen. All our friend's lectures, including sundry ones he gave out of town, were edited by one of the younger members of the German Department. The procedure was somewhat complicated. Professor Pnin laboriously translated his own Russian verbal flow, teeming with idiomatic proverbs, into patchy English. This was revised by young Miller. Then Dr. Hagen's secretary, a Miss Eisenbohr, typed it out. Then Pnin deleted the passages he could not understand. Then he read it to his weekly audience. He was utterly helpless without the prepared text, nor could he use the ancient system of dissimulating his infirmity by moving his eyes up and down—snapping up an eyeful of words, reeling them off to his audience, and drawing out the end of the sentence while diving for the next. Pnin's worried eye would be bound to lose its bearings. Therefore he preferred reading his lectures, his gaze glued to his text, in a slow, monotonous baritone that seemed to climb one of those interminable flights of stairs used by people who dread elevators.

The conductor, a gray-headed fatherly person with steel spectacles placed rather low on his simple, functional nose and a bit of soiled adhesive tape on his thumb, had now only three coaches to deal with before reaching the last one, where Pnin rode.

Pnin in the meantime had yielded to the satisfaction of a special Pninian craving. He was in a Pninian quandary. Among other articles indispensable for a Pninian overnight stay in a strange town, such as shoe trees, apples, dictionaries, and so on, his Gladstone bag contained a relatively new black suit he planned to wear that night for the lecture ("Are the Russian People Communist?") before the Cremona ladies. It also contained next Monday's symposium lecture ("Don Quixote and Faust"), which he intended to study the next day, on his way back to Waindell, and a paper by the graduate student, Betty Bliss ("Dostoevski and Gestalt Psychology"), that he had to read for Dr. Hagen, who was her main director of cerebration. The quandary was as follows: If he kept the Cremona manuscript—a sheaf of typewriter-size pages, carefully folded down the center—on his person, in the security of his body warmth, the chances were, theoretically, that he would forget to transfer it from the coat he was wearing to the one he would wear. On the other hand, if he placed the lecture in the pocket of the suit in the bag *now*, he would, he knew, be tortured by the possibility of his luggage being stolen. On the third hand (these mental states sprout additional forelimbs all the time), he carried in the inside pocket of his present coat a precious wallet with two ten-dollar bills, the newspaper clipping of a letter he had written, with my help, to the New York Times in 1945 anent the Yalta conference, and his certificate of naturalization; and it was physically possible to pull out the wallet, if needed, in such a way as fatally to dislodge the folded lecture. During the twenty minutes he had been on the train, our friend had already opened his bag twice to play with his various papers. When the conductor reached the car, diligent Pnin was perusing with difficulty Betty's last effort, which began, "When we consider the mental climate wherein we all live, we cannot but notice——"

The conductor entered; did not awake the soldier;

16

promised the women he would let them know when they would be about to arrive; and presently was shaking his head over Pnin's ticket. The Cremona stop had been abolished two years before.

"Important lecture!" cried Pnin. "What to do? It is a cata-stroph!"

Gravely, comfortably, the gray-headed conductor sank into the opposite seat and consulted in silence a tattered book full of dog-eared insertions. In a few minutes, namely at 3:08, Pnin would have to get off at Whitchurch; this would enable him to catch the four-o'clock bus that would deposit him, around six, at Cremona.

"I was thinking I gained twelve minutes, and now I have lost nearly two whole hours," said Pnin bitterly. Upon which, clearing his throat and ignoring the consolation offered by the kind gray-head ("You'll make it."), he took off his reading glasses, collected his stone-heavy bag, and repaired to the vestibule of the car so as to wait there for the confused greenery skimming by to be cancelled and replaced by the definite station he had in mind.

2

Whitchurch materialized as scheduled. A hot, torpid expanse of cement and sun lay beyond the geometrical solids of various clean-cut shadows. The local weather was unbelievably summery for October. Alert, Pnin entered a waiting room of sorts, with a needless stove in the middle, and looked around. In a solitary recess, one could make out the upper part of a perspiring young man who was filling out forms on the broad wooden counter before him.

"Information, please," said Pnin. "Where stops four-o'clock bus to Cremona?"

"Right across the street," briskly answered the employee without looking up.

"And where possible to leave baggage?"

"That bag? I'll take care of it."

And with the national informality that always nonplused Pnin, the young man shoved the bag into a corner of his nook.

"Quittance?" queried Pnin, Englishing the Russian for "receipt" (*kvitantsiya*).

"What's that?"

"Number?" tried Pnin.

"You don't need a number," said the fellow, and resumed his writing.

Pnin left the station, satisfied himself about the bus stop, and entered a coffee shop. He consumed a ham sandwich, ordered another, and consumed that too. At exactly five minutes to four, having paid for the food but not for an excellent toothpick which he carefully selected from a neat little cup in the shape of a pine cone near the cash register, Pnin walked back to the station for his bag.

A different man was now in charge. The first had been called home to drive his wife in all haste to the maternity hospital. He would be back in a few minutes.

"But I must obtain my valise!" cried Pnin.

The substitute was sorry but could not do a thing.

"It is there!" cried Pnin, leaning over and pointing.

This was unfortunate. He was still in the act of pointing when he realized that he was claiming the wrong bag. His index finger wavered. That hesitation was fatal.

"My bus to Cremona!" cried Pnin.

"There is another at eight," said the man.

What was our poor friend to do? Horrible situation! He glanced streetward. The bus had just come. The engagement meant an extra fifty dollars. His hand flew to his right side. *It* was there, *slava Bogu* (thank God)! Very well! He would not wear his black suit—*vot i vsyo* (that's all). He would retrieve it on his way back. He had lost, dumped, shed many more valuable things in his day. Energetically, almost lightheartedly, Pnin boarded the bus.

He had endured this new stage of his journey only for a few city blocks when an awful suspicion crossed his mind. Ever since he had been separated from his bag, the tip of his left forefinger had been alternating with the proximal edge of his right elbow in checking a precious presence in his inside coat pocket. All of a sudden he brutally yanked it out. It was Betty's paper.

Emitting what he thought were international exclamations of anxiety and entreaty, Pnin lurched out of his seat. Reeling, he reached the exit. With one hand the driver grimly milked out a handful of coins from his little machine, refunded him the price of the ticket, and stopped the bus. Poor Pnin landed in the middle of a strange town.

He was less strong than his powerfully puffed-out chest might imply, and the wave of hopeless fatigue that suddenly submerged his topheavy body, detaching him, as it were, from reality, was a sensation not utterly unknown to him. He found himself in a damp, green, purplish park, of the formal and funereal type, with the stress laid on somber rhododendrons, glossy laurels, sprayed shade trees and closely clipped lawns; and hardly had he turned into an alley of chestnut and oak, which the bus driver had curtly told him led back to the railway station, than that eerie feeling, that tingle of unreality overpowered him completely. Was it something he had eaten? That pickle with the ham? Was it a mysterious disease that none of his doctors had yet detected? My friend wondered, and I wonder, too.

I do not know if it has ever been noted before that one of the main characteristics of life is discreteness. Unless a film of flesh envelops us, we die. Man exists only insofar as he is separated from his surroundings. The cranium is a space-traveler's helmet. Stay inside or you perish. Death is divestment, death is communion. It may be wonderful to mix with the landscape, but to do so is the end of the tender ego. The sensation poor Pnin experienced was something very like that divestment, that communion. He felt porous and pregnable. He was sweating. He was terrified. A stone bench among the laurels saved him from collapsing on the sidewalk. Was his seizure a heart attack? I doubt it. For the nonce I am his physician, and let me repeat, I doubt it. My patient was one of those singular and unfortunate people who regard their heart ("a hollow, muscular organ," according to the gruesome definition in *Webster's New Collegiate Dictionary*, which Pnin's orphaned bag contained) with a queasy dread, a nervous repulsion, a sick hate, as if it were some strong slimy untouchable monster that one had to be parasitized with, alas. Occasionally, when puzzled by his tumbling and tottering pulse, doctors examined him more thoroughly, the cardiograph outlined fabulous mountain ranges and indicated a dozen fatal diseases that excluded one another. He was afraid of touching his own wrist. He never attempted to sleep on his left side, even in those dismal hours of the night when the insomniac longs for a third side after trying the two he has.

And now, in the park of Whitchurch, Pnin felt what he had felt already on August 10, 1942, and February 15 (his birthday), 1937, and May 18, 1929, and July 4, 1920—that the repulsive automaton he lodged had developed a consciousness of its own and not only was grossly alive but was causing him pain and panic. He pressed his poor bald head against the stone back of the bench and recalled all the past occasions of similar discomfort and despair. Could it be pneumonia this time? He had been chilled to the bone a couple of days before in one of those hearty American drafts that a host treats his guests to after the second round of drinks on a windy night. And suddenly Pnin (was he dying?) found himself sliding back into his own childhood. This sensation had the sharpness of retrospective detail that is said to be the dramatic privilege of drowning individuals, especially in the former Russian Navy—a phenomenon of suffocation that a veteran psychoanalyst, whose name escapes me, has explained as being the subconsciously evoked shock of one's baptism which causes an explosion of intervening recollections between the first immersion and the last. It all happened in a flash but there is no way of rendering it in less than so many consecutive words.

Pnin came from a respectable, fairly well-to-do, St. Petersburg family. His father, Dr. Pavel Pnin, an eye specialist of considerable repute, had once had the honor of treating Leo Tolstoy for a case of conjunctivitis. Timofey's mother, a frail, nervous little person with a waspy waist and bobbed hair, was the daughter of the once famous revolutionary Umov (rhymes with "zoom off") and of a German lady from Riga. Through his half swoon, he saw his mother's approaching eyes. It was a Sunday in midwinter. He was eleven. He had been preparing lessons for his Monday classes at the First Gymnasium when a strange chill pervaded his body. His mother took his temperature, looked at her child with a kind of stupefaction, and immediately called her husband's best friend, the pediatrician Belochkin. He was a small, beetle-browed man, with a short beard and cropped hair. Easing the skirts of his frock coat, he sat down on the edge of Timofey's bed. A race was run between the doctor's fat golden watch and Timofey's pulse (an easy winner). Then Timofey's torso was bared, and to it Belochkin pressed the icy nudity of his ear and the sandpapery side of his head. Like the flat sole of some monopode, the ear ambulated all over Timofey's back and chest, gluing itself to this or that patch of skin and stomping on to the next. No sooner had the doctor left than Timofey's mother and a robust servant girl with safety pins between her teeth encased the distressed little patient in a strait-jacket-like compress. It consisted of a layer of soaked linen, a thicker layer of absorbent cotton, and another of tight flannel, with a sticky diabolical oilcloth—the hue of urine and fever—coming between the clammy pang of the linen next to his skin and the excruciating squeak of the cotton around which the outer layer of flannel was wound. A poor cocooned pupa, Timosha (Tim) lay under a mass of additional blankets; they were of no avail against the branching chill that crept up his ribs from both sides of his frozen spine. He could not close his eyes because his eyelids stung so. Vision was but oval pain with oblique stabs of light; familiar shapes became the breeding places of evil delusions. Near his bed was a four-section screen of polished wood, with pyrographic designs representing a bridle path felted with fallen leaves, a lily pond, an old man hunched up on a bench, and a squirrel holding a reddish object in its front paws. Timosha, a methodical child, had often wondered what that object could be (a nut? a pine cone?), and now that he had nothing else to do, he set himself to solve this dreary riddle, but the fever that hummed in his head drowned every effort in pain and panic. Still more oppressive was his tussle with the wallpaper. He had always been able to see that in the vertical plane a combination made up of three different clusters of purple flowers and seven different oak leaves was repeated a number of times with soothing exactitude; but now he was bothered by the undismissable fact that he could not find what system of inclusion and circumscription governed the horizontal recurrence of the pattern; that such a recurrence existed was proved by his being able to pick out here and there, all along the wall from bed to wardrobe and from stove to door, the reappearance of this or that element of the series, but when he tried traveling right or left from any chosen set of three inflorescences and seven leaves, he forthwith lost himself in a meaningless tangle of rhododendron and oak. It stood to reason that if the evil designer—the destroyer of minds, the friend of fever—had concealed the key of the pattern with such monstrous care, that key must be as precious as life itself and, when found, would regain for Timofey Pnin his everyday health, his everyday world; and this lucid—alas, too lucid—thought forced him to persevere in the struggle.

A sense of being late for some appointment as odiously exact as school, dinner, or bedtime added the discomfort of awkward haste to the difficulties of a quest that was grading into delirium. The foliage and the flowers, with none of the intricacies of their warp disturbed, appeared to detach themselves in one undulating body from their pale-blue background which, in its turn, lost its papery flatness and dilated in depth till the spectator's heart almost burst in response to the expansion. He could still make out through the autonomous garlands certain parts of the nursery more tenacious of life than the rest, such as the lacquered screen, the gleam of a tumbler, the brass knobs of his bedstead, but these interfered even less with the oak leaves and rich blossoms than would the reflection of an inside object in a windowpane with the outside scenery perceived through the same glass. And although the witness and victim of these phantasms was tucked up in bed, he was, in accordance with the twofold nature of his surroundings, simultaneously seated on a bench in a green and purple park. During one melting moment, he had the sensation of holding at last the key he had sought; but, coming from very far, a rustling wind, its soft volume increasing as it ruffled the rhododendrons—now blossomless, blind—confused whatever rational pattern Timofey Pnin's surroundings had once had. He was alive and that was sufficient. The back of the bench against which he still sprawled felt as real as his clothes, or his wallet, or the date of the Great Moscow Fire—1812.

A gray squirrel sitting on comfortable haunches on

24

the ground before him was sampling a peach stone. The wind paused, and presently stirred the foliage again.

The seizure had left him a little frightened and shaky, but he argued that had it been a real heart attack, he would have surely felt a good deal more unsettled and concerned, and this roundabout piece of reasoning completely dispelled his fear. It was now four-twenty. He blew his nose and trudged to the station.

The initial employee was back. "Here's your bag," he said cheerfully. "Sorry you missed the Cremona bus."

"At least"—and what dignified irony our unfortunate friend tried to inject into that "at least"—"I hope everything is good with your wife?"

"She'll be all right. Have to wait till tomorrow, I guess."

"And now," said Pnin, "where is located the public telephone?"

The man pointed with his pencil as far out and sideways as he could without leaving his lair. Pnin, bag in hand, started to go, but he was called back. The pencil was now directed streetward.

"Say, see those two guys loading that truck? They're going to Cremona right now. Just tell them Bob Horn sent you. They'll take you."

3

Some people—and I am one of them—hate happy ends. We feel cheated. Harm is the norm. Doom should not jam. The avalanche stopping in its tracks a few feet above the cowering village behaves not only unnaturally but unethically. Had I been reading about this mild old man, instead of writing about him, I would have preferred him to discover, upon his arrival to Cremona, that his lecture was not this Friday but the next. Actually, however, he not only arrived safely but was in time for dinner—a fruit cocktail, to begin with, mint jelly with the anonymous meat course, chocolate syrup with the vanilla ice cream. And soon afterwards, surfeited with sweets, wearing his black suit, and juggling three papers, all of which he had stuffed into his coat so as to have the one he wanted among the rest (thus thwarting mischance by mathematical necessity), he sat on a chair near the lectern, while, at the lectern, Judith Clyde, an ageless blonde in aqua rayon, with large, flat cheeks stained a beautiful candy pink and two bright eyes basking in blue lunacy behind a rimless pince-nez, presented the speaker:

"Tonight," she said, "the speaker of the evening—— This, by the way, is our third Friday night; last time, as you all remember, we all enjoyed hearing what Professor Moore had to say about agriculture in China. Tonight we have here, I am proud to say, the Russian-born, and citizen of this country, Professor—now comes a difficult one, I am afraid—Professor Pun-neen. I hope I have it right. He hardly needs any introduction, of course, and we are all happy to have him. We have a long evening before us, a long and rewarding evening, and I am sure you would all like to have time to ask him questions afterwards. Incidentally, I am told his father was Dostoevski's family doctor, and he has traveled quite a bit on both sides of the Iron Curtain. Therefore I will not take up your precious time any longer and will only add a few words about our next

Friday lecture in this program. I am sure you will all be delighted to know that there is a grand surprise in store for all of us. Our next lecturer is the distinguished poet and prose writer, Miss Linda Lacefield. We all know she has written poetry, prose, and some short stories. Miss Lacefield was born in New York. Her ancestors on both sides fought on both sides in the Revolutionary War. She wrote her first poem before graduation. Many of her poems—three of them, at least—have been published in *Response, A Hundred Love Lyrics by American Women.* In 1922 she received the cash prize offered by——"

But Pnin was not listening. A faint ripple stemming from his recent seizure was holding his fascinated attention. It lasted only a few heartbeats, with an additional systole here and there—last, harmless echoes—and was resolved in demure reality as his distinguished hostess invited him to the lectern; but while it lasted, how limpid the vision was! In the middle of the front row of seats he saw one of his Baltic aunts, wearing the pearls and the lace and the blond wig she had worn at all the performances given by the great ham actor Khodotov, whom she had adored from afar before drifting into insanity. Next to her, shyly smiling, sleek dark head inclined, gentle brown gaze shining up at Pnin from under velvet eyebrows, sat a dead sweetheart of his, fanning herself with a program. Murdered, forgotten, unrevenged, incorrupt, immortal, many old friends were scattered throughout the dim hall among more recent people, such as Miss Clyde, who had modestly regained a front seat. Vanya Bednyashkin, shot by the Reds in 1919 in Odessa because his father had been a Liberal, was gaily signaling to his former schoolmate from the back of the hall. And in an inconspicuous situation Dr. Pavel Pnin and his anxious wife, both a little blurred but on the whole wonderfully recovered from their obscure dissolution, looked at their son with the same life-consuming passion and pride that they had looked at him with that night in 1912 when, at a school festival, commemorating Napoleon's defeat, he had recited (a bespectacled lad all alone on the stage) a poem by Pushkin.

The brief vision was gone. Old Miss Herring, retired Professor of History, author of *Russia Awakes* (1922), was bending across one or two intermediate members of the audience to compliment Miss Clyde on her speech, while from behind that lady another twinkling old party was thrusting into her field of vision a pair of withered, soundlessly clapping hands.

Chapter Two

1

The famous Waindell College bells were in the midst
of their morning chimes.

Laurence G. Clements, a Waindell scholar, whose
only popular course was the Philosophy of Gesture, and
his wife Joan, Pendelton '30, had recently parted with
their daughter, her father's best student: Isabel had
married in her junior year a Waindell graduate with
an engineering job in a remote Western State.

The bells were musical in the silvery sun. Framed
in the picture window, the little town of Waindell—
white paint, black pattern of twigs—was projected, as
if by a child, in primitive perspective devoid of aerial

depth, into the slate-gray hills; everything was prettily frosted with rime; the shiny parts of parked cars shone; Miss Dingwall's old Scotch terrier, a cylindrical small boar of sorts, had started upon his rounds up Warren Street and down Spelman Avenue and back again; but no amount of neighborliness, landscaping, and change ringing could soften the season; in a fortnight, after a ruminant pause, the academic year would enter its most winterly phase, the Spring Term, and the Clementses felt dejected, apprehensive, and lonely in their nice old drafty house that now seemed to hang about them like the flabby skin and flapping clothes of some fool who had gone and lost a third of his weight. Isabel was so young after all, and so vague, and they really knew nothing about her in-laws beyond that wedding selection of marchpane faces in a hired hall with the vaporous bride so helpless without her glasses.

The bells, under the enthusiastic direction of Dr. Robert Trebler, active member of the Music Department, were still going strong in the angelic sky, and over a frugal breakfast of oranges and lemons Laurence, blondish, baldish, and unwholesomely fat, was criticizing the head of the French Department, one of the people Joan had invited to meet Professor Entwistle of Goldwin University at their house that evening. "Why on earth," he fumed, "did you have to ask that fellow Blorenge, a mummy, a bore, one of the stucco pillars of education?"

"I *like* Ann Blorenge," said Joan, stressing her affirmation and affection with nods. "A vulgar old cat!" cried Laurence. "A pathetic old cat," murmured Joan—and it was then that Dr. Trebler stopped and the hallway telephone took over.

Technically speaking, the narrator's art of integrating telephone conversations still lags far behind that of rendering dialogues conducted from room to room, or from window to window across some narrow blue alley in an ancient town with water so precious, and the misery of donkeys, and rugs for sale, and minarets, and foreigners and melons, and the vibrant morning echoes. When Joan, in her brisk long-limbed way, got to the compelling instrument before it gave up, and said hullo (eyebrows up, eyes roaming), a hollow quiet greeted her; all she could hear was the informal sound of a steady breathing; presently the breather's voice said, with a cozy foreign accent: "One moment, excuse me"—this was quite casual, and he continued to breathe and perhaps hem and hum or even sigh a little to the accompaniment of a crepitation that evoked the turning over of small pages.

"Hullo!" she repeated.

"You are," suggested the voice warily, "Mrs. Fire?"

"No," said Joan, and hung up. "And besides," she went on, swinging back into the kitchen and addressing her husband who was sampling the bacon she had prepared for herself, "you cannot deny that Jack Cockerell considers Blorenge to be a first-rate administrator."

"What was that telephone call?"

"Somebody wanting Mrs. Feuer or Fayer. Look here, if you deliberately neglect everything George——" [Dr. O. G. Helm, their family doctor]

"Joan," said Laurence, who felt much better after that opalescent rasher, "Joan, my dear, you are aware, aren't you, that you told Margaret Thayer yesterday you wanted a roomer?"

"Oh, gosh," said Joan—and obligingly the telephone rang again.

"It is evident," said the same voice, comfortably resuming the conversation, "that I employed by mistake the name of the informer. I am connected with Mrs. Clement?"

"Yes, this is Mrs. Clements," said Joan.

"Here speaks Professor——" There followed a preposterous little explosion. "I conduct the classes in Russian. Mrs. Fire, who is now working at the library part time——"

"Yes—Mrs. Thayer, I know. Well, do you want to see that room?"

He did. Could he come to inspect it in approximately half an hour? Yes, she would be in. Untenderly she cradled the receiver.

"What was it this time?" asked her husband, looking back, pudgy freckled hand on banister, on his way upstairs to the security of his study.

"A cracked ping-pong ball. Russian."

"Professor Pnin, by God!" cried Laurence. " 'I know him well: he is the brooch——' Well, I flatly refuse to have that freak in my house."

He trudged up, truculently. She called after him:

"Lore, did you finish writing that article last night?"

"Almost." He had turned the corner of the stairs—she heard his hand squeaking on the banisters, then striking them. "I will today. First I have that damned EOS examination to prepare."

This stood for the Evolution of Sense, his greatest course (with an enrollment of twelve, none even remotely apostolic) which had opened and would close with the phrase destined to be overquoted one day:

The evolution of sense is, in a sense, the evolution of nonsense.

2

Half an hour later, Joan glanced over the moribund cactuses in the sun-porch window and saw a raincoated, hatless man, with a head like a polished globe of copper, optimistically ringing at the front door of her neighbor's beautiful brick house. The old Scotty stood beside him in much the same candid attitude as he. Miss Dingwall came out with a mop, let the slowpoke, dignified dog in, and directed Pnin to the Clements' clapboard residence.

Timofey Pnin settled down in the living room, crossed his legs *po amerikanski* (the American way), and entered into some unnecessary detail. It was a curriculum vitae in a nutshell—a coconut shell. Born in St. Petersburg in 1898. Both parents died of typhus in 1917. Left for Kiev in 1918. Was with the White Army five months, first as a "field telephonist," then at the Military Information Office. Escaped from Red-invaded Crimea to Constantinople in 1919. Completed university education——

"Say, I was there as a child exactly the same year," said pleased Joan. "My father went to Turkey on a government mission and took us along. We might have met! I remember the word for water. And there was a rose garden——"

"Water in Turkish is 'su,'" said Pnin, a linguist by necessity, and went on with his fascinating past: Completed university education in Prague. Was connected with various scientific institutions. Then—— "Well, to make a long story very short: habitated in Paris from

1925, abandoned France at beginning of Hitler war. Is now here. Is American citizen. Is teaching Russian and such like subjects at Vandal College. From Hagen, Head of German Department, obtainable all references. Or from the College Home for Single Instructors."

Hadn't he been comfortable there?

"Too many people," said Pnin. "Inquisitive people. Whereas special privacy is now to me absolutely necessary." He coughed into his fist with an unexpected cavernous sound (which somehow reminded Joan of a professional Don Cossack she had once met) and then took the plunge: "I must warn: will have all my teeth pulled out. It is a repulsive operation."

"Well, come upstairs," said Joan brightly.

Pnin peered into Isabel's pink-walled, white-flounced room. It had suddenly begun to snow, though the sky was pure platinum, and the slow scintillant downcome got reflected in the silent looking glass. Methodically Pnin inspected Hoecker's "Girl with a Cat" above the bed, and Hunt's "The Belated Kid" above the bookshelf. Then he held his hand at a little distance from the window.

"Is temperature uniform?"

Joan dashed to the radiator.

"Piping hot," she reported.

"I am asking—are there currents of air?"

"Oh yes, you will have plenty of air. And here is the bathroom—small, but all yours."

"No *douche*?" inquired Pnin, looking up. "Maybe it is better so. My friend, Professor Chateau of Columbia, once broke his leg in two places. Now I must think. What price are you prepared to demand? I ask it,

34

because I will not give more than a dollar per day—not including, of course, nootrition."

"All right," said Joan with that pleasant, quick laugh of hers.

The same afternoon, one of Pnin's students, Charles McBeth ("A madman, I think, judging by his compositions," Pnin used to say), zestfully brought over Pnin's luggage in a pathologically purplish car with no fenders on the left side, and after an early dinner at The Egg and We, a recently inaugurated and not very successful little restaurant which Pnin frequented from sheer sympathy with failure, our friend applied himself to the pleasant task of Pninizing his new quarters. Isabel's adolescence had gone with her, or, if not, had been eradicated by her mother, but traces of the girl's childhood somehow had been allowed to remain, and before finding the most advantageous situations for his elaborate sun lamp, huge Russian-alphabet typewriter in a broken coffin fixed with Scotch tape, five pairs of handsome, curiously small shoes with ten shoe trees rooted in them, a coffee grinding-and-boiling contraption which was not quite as good as the one that had exploded last year, a couple of alarm clocks running the same race every night, and seventy-four library books, mainly old Russian periodicals solidly bound by WCL, Pnin delicately exiled to a chair on the landing half a dozen forlorn volumes, such as *Birds at Home, Happy Days in Holland*, and *My First Dictionary* ("With more than 600 illustrations depicting zoos, the human body, farms, fires—all scientifically chosen"), and also a lone wooden bead with a hole through the center.

Joan, who used the word "pathetic" perhaps a little too often, declared she would ask that pathetic savant for a drink with their guests, to which her husband replied he was also a pathetic savant and would go to a movie if she carried out her threat. However, when Joan went up to Pnin with her offer he declined the invitation, saying, rather simply, he had resolved not to use alcohol any more. Three couples and Entwistle arrived around nine, and by ten the little party was in full swing, when suddenly Joan, while talking to pretty Gwen Cockerell, noticed Pnin, in a green sweater, standing in the doorway that led to the foot of the stairs and holding aloft, for her to see, a tumbler. She sped toward him—and simultaneously her husband almost collided with her as he trotted across the room to stop, choke, abolish Jack Cockerell, head of the English Department, who, with his back to Pnin, was entertaining Mrs. Hagen and Mrs. Blorenge with his famous act— he being one of the greatest, if not the greatest, mimics of Pnin on the campus. His model, in the meantime, was saying to Joan: "This is not a clean glass in the bathroom, and there exist other troubles. It blows from the floor, and it blows from the walls——" But Dr. Hagen, a pleasant, rectangular old man, had noticed Pnin, too, and was greeting him joyfully, and the next moment Pnin, his tumbler replaced by a highball, was being introduced to Professor Entwistle.

"*Zdrastvuyte kak pozhivaete horosho spasibo,*" Entwistle rattled off in excellent imitation of Russian speech—and indeed he rather resembled a genial Tsarist colonel in mufti. "One night in Paris," he went on, his eyes twinkling, "at the *Ougolok* cabaret, this demonstration convinced a group of Russian revelers that I was a compatriot of theirs—posing as an American, don't you know."

"In two-three years," said Pnin, missing one bus but boarding the next, "I will also be taken for an American," and everybody roared except Professor Blorenge.

"We'll get you an electric heater," Joan told Pnin confidentially, as she offered him some olives.

"What make heater?" asked Pnin suspiciously.

"That remains to be seen. Any other complaints?"

"Yes—sonic disturbance," said Pnin. "I hear every, every sound from downstairs, but now it is not the place to discuss it, I think."

3

The guests started to leave. Pnin trudged upstairs, a clean glass in his hand. Entwistle and his host were the last to come out on the porch. Wet snow drifted in the black night.

"It's such a pity," said Professor Entwistle, "that we cannot tempt you to come to Goldwin for good. We have Schwarz and old Crates, who are among your greatest admirers. We have a real lake. We have everything. We even have a Professor Pnin on our staff."

"I know, I know," said Clements, "but these offers I keep getting are coming too late. I plan to retire soon, and till then I prefer to remain in the musty but familiar hole. How did you like"—he lowered his voice—"Monsieur Blorenge?"

"Oh, he struck me as a capital fellow. In some ways, however, I must say he reminded me of that probably legendary figure, the Chairman of French, who thought Chateaubriand was a famous *chef*."

"Careful," said Clements. "That story was first told about Blorenge, and is true."

Next morning heroic Pnin marched to town, walking a cane in the European manner (up-down, up-down) and letting his gaze dwell upon various objects in a philosophical effort to imagine what it would be to see them again after the ordeal and then recall what it had been to perceive them through the prism of its expectation. Two hours later he was trudging back, leaning on his cane and not looking at anything. A warm flow of pain was gradually replacing the ice and wood of the anesthetic in his thawing, still half-dead, abominably martyred mouth. After that, during a few days he was in mourning for an intimate part of himself. It surprised him to realize how fond he had been of his teeth. His tongue, a fat sleek seal, used to flop and slide so happily among the familiar rocks, checking the contours of a battered but still secure kingdom, plunging from cave to cove, climbing this jag, nuzzling that notch, finding a shred of sweet seaweed in the same old cleft; but now not a landmark remained, and all there existed was a great dark wound, a terra incognita of gums which dread and disgust forbade one to investigate. And when the plates were thrust in, it was like a poor fossil skull being fitted with the grinning jaws of a perfect stranger.

There were, as per plan, no lectures, nor did he attend the examinations given for him by Miller. Ten days passed—and suddenly he began to enjoy the new gadget. It was a revelation, it was a sunrise, it was a firm mouthful of efficient, alabastrine, humane America. At night he kept his treasure in a special glass of special fluid where it smiled to itself, pink and pearly, as perfect as some lovely representative of deep-sea flora. The great work on Old Russia, a wonderful dream mixture of folklore, poetry, social history, and *petite histoire*, which for the last ten years or so he had been fondly planning, now seemed accessible at last, with headaches gone, and this new amphitheater of translucid plastics implying, as it were, a stage and a performance. When the spring term began his class could not help noticing the sea change, as he sat coquettishly tapping with the rubber end of a pencil upon those even, too even, incisors and canines while some student translated some sentence in old and ruddy Professor Oliver Bradstreet Mann's *Elementary Russian* (actually written from beginning to end by two frail drudges, John and Olga Krotki, both dead today), such as "The boy is playing with his nurse and his uncle." And one evening he waylaid Laurence Clements, who was in the act of scuttling up to his study, and with incoherent exclamations of triumph started to demonstrate the beauty of the thing, the ease with which it could be taken out and put in again, and urged surprised but not unfriendly Laurence to have all his teeth out first thing tomorrow.

"You will be a reformed man like I," cried Pnin.

It should be said for both Laurence and Joan that rather soon they began to appreciate Pnin at his unique Pninian worth, and this despite the fact that he was more of a poltergeist than a lodger. He did something fatal to his new heater and gloomily said never mind, it would soon be spring now. He had an irritating way of standing on the landing and assiduously brushing his clothes there, the brush clinking against the buttons, for at least five minutes every blessed morning. He had a passionate intrigue with Joan's washing machine. Although forbidden to come near it, he would be caught trespassing again and again. Casting aside all decorum and caution, he would feed it anything that happened to be at hand, his handkerchief, kitchen towels, a heap of shorts and shirts smuggled down from his room, just for the joy of watching through that porthole what looked like an endless tumble of dolphins with the staggers. One Sunday, after checking the solitude, he could not resist, out of sheer scientific curiosity, giving the mighty machine a pair of rubber-soled canvas shoes stained with clay and chlorophyll to play with; the shoes tramped away with a dreadful arhythmic sound, like an army going over a bridge, and came back without their soles, and Joan appeared from her little sitting room behind the pantry and said in sadness, "Again, Timofey?" But she forgave him, and liked to sit with him at the kitchen table, both cracking nuts or drinking tea. Desdemona, the old colored charwoman, who came on Fridays and with whom at one time God had gossiped daily ("'Desdemona,' the Lord would say to me, 'that man George is no good.'"), happened to glimpse Pnin basking in the unearthly lilac light of his sun lamp, wearing nothing but shorts, dark glasses, and a dazzling Greek-Catholic cross on his broad chest, and insisted thereafter that he was a saint. Laurence, on going up to his study one day, a secret and sacred lair cunningly carved out of the attic, was incensed to find the mellow lights on and fat-naped Pnin braced on his thin legs serenely browsing in a corner: "Excuse me, I only am grazing," as the gentle intruder (whose English was growing richer at a surprising pace) remarked, glancing over the higher of his two shoulders;

but somehow that very afternoon a chance reference to a rare author, a passing allusion tacitly recognized in the middle distance of an idea, an adventurous sail descried on the horizon, led insensibly to a tender mental concord between the two men, both of whom were really at ease only in their warm world of natural scholarship. There are human solids and there are human surds, and Clements and Pnin belonged to the latter variety. Thenceforth they would often devise, as they met and stopped on thresholds, on landings, on two different levels of staircase steps (exchanging altitudes and turning to each other anew), or as they walked in opposite directions up and down a room which at the moment existed for them only as an *espace meublé*, to use a Pninian term. It soon transpired that Timofey was a veritable encyclopedia of Russian shrugs and shakes, had tabulated them, and could add something to Laurence's files on the philosophical interpretation of pictorial and non-pictorial, national and environmental gestures. It was very pleasant to see the two men discuss a legend or a religion, Timofey blossoming out in amphoric motion, Laurence chopping away with one hand. Laurence even made a film of what Timofey considered to be the essentials of Russian "carpalistics," with Pnin in a polo shirt, a Gioconda smile on his lips, demonstrating the movements underlying such Russian verbs—used in reference to hands—as *mahnut'*, *vsplesnut'*, *razvesti:* the one-hand downward loose shake of weary relinquishment; the two-hand dramatic splash of amazed distress; and the "disjunctive" motion —hands traveling apart to signify helpless passivity. And in conclusion, very slowly, Pnin showed how, in the international "shaking the finger" gesture, a half

41

turn, as delicate as the switch of the wrist in fencing, metamorphosed the Russian solemn symbol of pointing up, "the Judge in Heaven sees you!" into a German air picture of the stick—"something is coming to you!" "However," added objective Pnin, "Russian metaphysical police can break physical bones also very well."

With apologies for his "negligent toilet," Pnin showed the film to a group of students—and Betty Bliss, a graduate working in Comparative Literature where Pnin was assisting Dr. Hagen, announced that Timofey Pavlovich looked exactly like Buddha in an oriental moving picture she had seen in the Asiatic Department. This Betty Bliss, a plump maternal girl of some twenty-nine summers, was a soft thorn in Pnin's aging flesh. Ten years before she had had a handsome heel for a lover, who had jilted her for a little tramp, and later she had had a dragging, hopelessly complicated, Chekhovian rather than Dostoevskian affair with a cripple who was now married to his nurse, a cheap cutie. Poor Pnin hesitated. In principle, marriage was not excluded. In his new dental glory, he went so far one seminar session, after the rest had gone, as to hold her hand on his palm and pat it while they were sitting together and discussing Turgenev's poem in prose: "How fair, how fresh were the roses." She could hardly finish reading, her bosom bursting with sighs, the held hand aquiver. "Turgenev," said Pnin, putting the hand back on the table, "was made by the ugly, but adored by him, singer Pauline Viardot to play the idiot in charades and *tableaux vivants*, and Madam Pushkin said: 'You annoy me with your verses, Pushkin'—and in old age—to think only!—the wife of colossus, colossus

Tolstoy liked much better than him a stoopid moozishan with a red noz!"

Pnin had nothing against Miss Bliss. In trying to visualize a serene senility, he saw her with passable clarity bringing him his lap robe or refilling his fountain pen. He liked her all right—but his heart belonged to another woman.

The cat, as Pnin would say, cannot be hid in a bag. In order to explain my poor friend's abject excitement one evening in the middle of the term—when he received a certain telegram and then paced his room for at least forty minutes—it should be stated that Pnin had not always been single. The Clementses were playing Chinese checkers among the reflections of a comfortable fire when Pnin came clattering downstairs, slipped, and almost fell at their feet like a supplicant in some ancient city full of injustice, but retrieved his balance—only to crash into the poker and tongs.

"I have come," he said, panting, "to inform, or more correctly ask you, if I can have a female visitor Saturday—in the day, of course. She is my former wife, now Dr. Liza Wind—maybe you have heard in psychiatric circles."

5

There are some beloved women whose eyes, by a chance blend of brilliancy and shape, affect us not directly, not at the moment of shy perception, but in a delayed and cumulative burst of light when the heartless person is absent, and the magic agony abides, and its lenses and lamps are installed in the dark. Whatever eyes Liza Pnin, now Wind, had, they seemed to reveal their essence, their precious-stone water, only when you evoked them in thought, and then a blank, blind, moist aquamarine blaze shivered and stared as if a spatter of sun and sea had got between your own eyelids. Actually her eyes were of a light transparent blue with contrasting black lashes and bright pink canthus, and they slightly stretched up templeward, where a set of feline little lines fanned out from each. She had a sweep of dark brown hair above a lustrous forehead, and a snow-and-rose complexion, and she used a very light red lipstick, and save for a certain thickness of ankle and wrist, there was hardly a flaw to her full-blown, animated, elemental, not particularly well-groomed beauty.

Pnin, then a rising young scholar and she, a more limpid mermaid than now but practically the same person, had met around 1925, in Paris. He wore a sparse auburn beard (today only white bristles would sprout if he did not shave—poor Pnin, poor albino porcupine!), and this divided monastic growth, topped by a fat glossy nose and innocent eyes, nicely epitomized the physique of old-fashioned intellectual Russia. A small job at the Aksakov Institute, rue Vert-Vert, combined with another at Saul Bagrov's Russian book shop, rue Gresset, supplied him with a livelihood. Liza Bogolepov, a medical student just turned twenty, and perfectly charming in her black silk jumper and tailor-made skirt, was already working at the Meudon sanatorium directed by that remarkable and formidable old lady, Dr. Rosetta Stone, one of the most destructive psychiatrists of the day; and, moreover, Liza wrote verse— mainly in halting anapaest; indeed, Pnin saw her for the first time at one of those literary soirees where young émigré poets, who had left Russia in their pale, unpampered pubescence, chanted nostalgic elegies dedicated to a country that could be little more to them than a sad stylized toy, a bauble found in the attic, a crystal globe which you shake to make a soft luminous snowstorm inside over a minuscule fir tree and a log cabin of papier mâché. Pnin wrote her a tremendous love letter—now safe in a private collection—and she read it with tears of self pity while recovering from a pharmacopoeial attempt at suicide because of a rather silly affair with a littérateur who is now— But no matter. Five analysts, intimate friends of hers, all said: "Pnin—and a baby at once."

Marriage hardly changed their manner of life except that she moved into Pnin's dingy apartment. He went on with his Slavic studies, she with her psychodramatics and her lyrical ovipositing, laying all over the place like an Easter rabbit, and in those green and mauve poems— about the child she wanted to bear, and the lovers she wanted to have, and St. Petersburg (courtesy Anna Akhmatov)—every intonation, every image, every simile had been used before by other rhyming rabbits. One of her admirers, a banker, and straightforward patron of the arts, selected among the Parisian Russians an influential literary critic, Zhorzhik Uranski, and for a champagne dinner at the *Ougolok* had the old boy devote his next *feuilleton* in one of the Russian-language newspapers to an appreciation of Liza's muse on whose chestnut curls Zhorzhik calmly placed Anna Akhmatov's coronet, whereupon Liza burst into happy tears—for all the world like little Miss Michigan or the Oregon Rose Queen. Pnin, who was not in the know, carried about a folded clipping of that shameless rave in his honest pocketbook, naïvely reading out passages to this or that

45

amused friend until it got quite frayed and smudgy. Nor was he in the know concerning graver matters, and in fact was actually pasting the remnants of the review in an album when, on a December day in 1938, Liza telephoned from Meudon, saying that she was going to Montpellier with a man who understood her "organic ego," a Dr. Eric Wind, and would never see Timofey again. An unknown French woman with red hair called for Liza's things and said, well, you cellar rat, there is no more any poor lass to *taper dessus*—and a month or two later there dribbled in from Dr. Wind a German letter of sympathy and apology assuring *lieber Herr Pnin* that he, Dr. Wind, was eager to marry "the woman who has come out of your life into mine." Pnin of course would have given her a divorce as readily as he would his life, with the wet stems cut and a bit of fern, and all of it wrapped up as crisply as at the earth-smelling florist's when the rain makes gray and green mirrors of Easter day; but it transpired that in South America Dr. Wind had a wife with a tortuous mind and a phony passport, who did not wish to be bothered until certain plans of her own took shape. Meanwhile the New World had started to beckon Pnin too: from New York a great friend of his, Professor Konstantin Chateau, offered him every assistance for a migratory voyage. Pnin informed Dr. Wind of his plans and sent Liza the last issue of an émigré magazine where she was mentioned on page 202. He was halfway through the dreary hell that had been devised by European bureaucrats (to the vast amusement of the Soviets) for holders of that miserable thing, the Nansen Passport (a kind of parolee's card issued to Russian émigrés), when one damp April day in 1940 there was a vigorous ring at his door and Liza tramped in, puffing and carrying before her like a chest of drawers a seven-month pregnancy, and announced, as she tore off her hat and kicked off her shoes, that it had all been a mistake, and from now on she was again Pnin's faithful and lawful wife, ready to follow him wherever he went—even beyond the ocean if need be. Those days were probably the happiest in Pnin's life— it was a permanent glow of weighty, painful felicity— and the vernalization of the visas, and the preparations, and the medical examination, with a deaf-and-dumb doctor applying a dummy stethoscope to Pnin's jammed heart through all his clothes, and the kind Russian lady (a relative of mine) who was so helpful at the American Consulate, and the journey to Bordeaux, and the beautiful clean ship—everything had a rich fairy-tale tinge to it. He was not only ready to adopt the child when it came but was passionately eager to do so, and she listened with a satisfied, somewhat cowish expression to the pedagogical plans he unfolded, for he actually seemed to forehear the babe's vagitus, and its first word in the near future. She had always been fond of sugar-coated almonds, but now she consumed fabulous quantities of them (two pounds between Paris and Bordeaux), and ascetic Pnin contemplated her greed with shakes and shrugs of delighted awe, and something about the smooth silkiness of those *dragées* remained in his mind, forever mingled with the memory of her taut skin, her complexion, her flawless teeth.

It was a little disappointing that as soon as she came aboard she gave one glance at the swelling sea, said: "*Nu, eto izvinite* (Nothing doing)," and promptly retired into the womb of the ship, within which, for most of the crossing, she kept lying on her back in the cabin she shared with the loquacious wives of the three laconic Poles—a wrestler, a gardener, and a barber—whom Pnin got as cabin mates. On the third evening of the voyage, having remained in the lounge long after Liza had gone to sleep, he cheerfully accepted a game of chess proposed by the former editor of a Frankfurt newspaper, a melancholy baggy-eyed patriarch in a turtle-neck sweater and plus fours. Neither was a good player; both were addicted to spectacular but quite unsound sacrifices of pieces; each was overanxious to win; and the proceedings were furthermore enlivened by Pnin's fantastic brand of German (*"Wenn Sie so, dann ich so, und Pferd fliegt"*). Presently another passenger came up, said *entschuldigen Sie,* could he watch their game? And sat down beside them. He had reddish hair cropped close and long pale eyelashes resembling fish moths, and he wore a shabby double-breasted coat, and soon he was clucking under his breath and shaking his head every time the patriarch, after much dignified meditation, lurched forward to make a wild move. Finally this helpful spectator, obviously an expert, could not resist pushing back a pawn his compatriot had just moved, and pointing with a vibrating index to a rook instead—which the old Frankfurter incontinently drove into the armpit of Pnin's defense. Our man lost, of course, and was about to leave the lounge when the expert overtook him, saying *entschuldigen Sie,* could he talk for a moment to Herr Pnin? ("You see, I know your name," he remarked parenthetically, lifting his useful index)—and suggested a couple of beers at the bar. Pnin accepted, and when the tankards were placed before them the polite stranger continued thus: "In life, as in chess, it is always better to analyze one's motives and

48

intentions. The day we came on board I was like a playful child. Next morning, however, I began already to fear that an astute husband—this is not a compliment, but a hypothesis in retrospection—would sooner or later study the passenger list. Today my conscience has tried me and found me guilty. I can endure the deception no longer. Your health. This is not at all our German nectar but it is better than Coca-Cola. My name is Dr. Eric Wind; alas, it is not unknown to you."

Pnin, in silence, his face working, one palm still on the wet bar, had started to slither clumsily off his uncomfortable mushroom seat, but Wind put five long sensitive fingers on his sleeve.

"*Lasse mich, lasse mich,*" wailed Pnin, trying to beat off the limp fawning hand.

"Please!" said Dr. Wind. "Be just. The prisoner has always the last word; it is his right. Even the Nazis admit it. And first of all—I want you to allow me to pay at least one half of the lady's passage."

"*Ach nein, nein, nein,*" said Pnin. "Let us finish this nightmare conversation (*diese koschmarische Sprache*)."

"As you like," said Dr. Wind, and proceeded to impress upon pinned Pnin the following points: That it had all been Liza's idea—"simplifying matters, you know, for the sake of our child" (the "our" sounded tripersonal); that Liza should be treated as a very sick woman (pregnancy being really the sublimation of a death wish); that he (Dr. Wind) would marry her in America—"where I am also going," Dr. Wind added for clarity; and that he (Dr. Wind) should at least be permitted to pay for the beer. From then on to the end of the voyage that had turned from green and silver to a uniform gray, Pnin busied himself overtly with his English-language manuals, and although immutably meek with Liza, tried to see her as little as he could without awakening her suspicions. Every now and then Dr. Wind would appear from nowhere and make from afar signs of recognition and reassurance. And at last, when the great statue arose from the morning haze where, ready to be ignited by the sun, pale, spellbound buildings stood like those mysterious rectangles of unequal height that you see in bar graph representations of compared percentages (natural resources, the frequency of mirages in different deserts), Dr. Wind resolutely walked up to the Pnins and identified himself—"because all three of us must enter the land of liberty with pure hearts." And after a bathetic sojourn on Ellis Island, Timofey and Liza parted.

There were complications—but at last Wind married her. In the course of the first five years in America, Pnin glimpsed her on several occasions in New York; he and the Winds were naturalized on the same day; then, after his removal to Waindell in 1945, half a dozen years passed without any meetings or correspondence. He heard of her, however, from time to time. Recently (in December 1951) his friend Chateau had sent him an issue of a journal of psychiatry with an article written by Dr. Albina Dunkelberg, Dr. Eric Wind, and Dr. Liza Wind on "Group Psychotherapy Applied to Marriage Counseling." Pnin used to be always embarrassed by Liza's *"psihooslinie"* ("psychoasinine") interests, and even now, when he ought to have been indifferent, he felt a twinge of revulsion and pity. Eric and she were working under the great Bernard Maywood, a genial giant of a man—referred to as "The Boss" by over-

adaptive Eric—at a Research Bureau attached to a
Planned Parenthood Center. Encouraged by his and his
wife's protector, Eric evolved the ingenious idea (pos-
sibly not his own) of sidetracking some of the more
plastic and stupid clients of the Center into a psychotherapeutic trap—a "tension-releasing" circle on the lines
of a quilting bee, where young married women in groups
of eight relaxed in a comfortable room amid an atmosphere of cheerful first-name informality, with doctors at a table facing the group, and a secretary unob-
trusively taking notes, and traumatic episodes floating
out of everybody's childhood like corpses. At these sessions, the ladies were made to discuss among themselves with absolute frankness their problems of marital
maladjustment, which entailed, of course, comparing
notes on their mates, who later were interviewed, too,
in a special "husband group," likewise very informal,
with a great passing around of cigars and anatomic
charts. Pnin skipped the actual reports and case his-
tories—and there is no need to go here into those hilari-
ous details. Suffice it to say that already at the third session of the female group, after this or that lady had
gone home and seen the light and come back to de-
scribe the newly discovered sensation to her still blocked
but rapt sisters, a ringing note of revivalism pleasingly
colored the proceedings ("Well, girls, when George last
night——") And this was not all. Dr. Eric Wind hoped
to work out a technique that would allow bringing all
those husbands and wives together in a joint group. Incidentally it was deadening to hear him and Liza
smacking their lips over the word "group." In a long
letter to distressed Pnin, Professor Chateau affirmed
that Dr. Wind even called Siamese twins "a group."

51

And indeed progressive, idealistic Wind dreamed of a happy world consisting of Siamese centuplets, anatomically conjoined communities, whole nations built around a communicating liver. "It is nothing but a kind of microcosmos of communism—all that psychiatry," rumbled Pnin, in his answer to Chateau. "Why not leave their private sorrows to people? Is sorrow not, one asks, the only thing in the world people really possess?"

6

"Look," said Joan Saturday morning to her husband, "I have decided to tell Timofey they will have the house to themselves today from two to five. We must give those pathetic creatures every possible chance. There are things I can do in town, and you will be dropped at the library."

"It so happens," answered Laurence, "that I have not the least intention to be dropped or otherwise moved anywhere today. Besides, it is highly improbable they will need eight rooms for their reunion."

Pnin put on his new brown suit (paid for by the Cremona lecture) and, after a hurried lunch at The Egg and We, walked through the snow-patched park to the Waindell bus station, arriving there almost an hour too early. He did not bother to puzzle out why exactly Liza had felt the urgent need to see him on her way back from visiting St. Bartholomew's, the preparatory school near Boston that her son would go to next fall: all he knew was that a flood of happiness foamed and rose behind the invisible barrier that was to burst open any moment now. He met five buses, and in each of them clearly made out Liza waving to him through a window as she and the other passengers started to file out, and then one bus after another was drained and she had not turned up. Suddenly he heard her sonorous voice (*"Timofey, zdrastvuy!"*) behind him, and, wheeling around, saw her emerge from the only Greyhound he had decided would not bring her. What change could our friend discern in her? What change could there be, good God! There she was. She always felt hot and buoyant, no matter the cold, and now her sealskin coat was wide open on her frilled blouse as she hugged Pnin's head and he felt the grapefruit fragrance of her neck, and kept muttering: *"Nu, nu, vot i horosho, nu vot"*—mere verbal heart props—and she cried out: "Oh, he has splendid new teeth!" He helped her into a taxi, her bright diaphanous scarf caught on something, and Pnin slipped on the pavement, and the taximan said "Easy," and took her bag from him, and everything had happened before, in this exact sequence.

It was, she told him as they drove up Park Street, a school in the English tradition. No, she did not want to eat anything, she had had a big lunch at Albany. It was a "very fancy" school—she said this in English—the boys played a kind of indoor tennis with their hands, between walls, and there would be in his form a —— (she produced with false nonchalance a well-known American name which meant nothing to Pnin because it was not that of a poet or a president). "By the way," interrupted Pnin, ducking and pointing, "you can just see a corner of the campus from here." All this was due ("Yes, I see, *vizhu, vizhu, kampus kak kampus:* The usual kind of thing"), all this, including a scholarship, was due to the influence of Dr. Maywood ("You know, Timofey, some day you should write him a word, just a

53

little sign of courtesy"). The Principal, a clergyman, had shown her the trophies Bernard had won there as a boy. Eric of course had wanted Victor to go to a public school but had been overruled. The Reverend Hopper's wife was the niece of an English Earl.

"Here we are. This is my *palazzo*," said jocose Pnin, who had not been able to concentrate on her rapid speech.

They entered—and he suddenly felt that this day which he had been looking forward to with such fierce longing was passing much too quickly—was going, going, would be gone in a few minutes. Perhaps, he thought, if she said right away what she wanted of him the day might slow down and be really enjoyed.

"What a gruesome place, *kakoy zhutkiy dom*," she said, sitting on the chair near the telephone and taking off her galoshes—such familiar movements! "Look at that aquarelle with the minarets. They must be terrible people."

"No," said Pnin, "they are my friends."

"My dear Timofey," she said, as he escorted her upstairs, "you have had some pretty awful friends in your time."

"And here is my room," said Pnin.

"I think I'll lie on your virgin bed, Timofey. And I'll recite you some verses in a minute. That hellish headache of mine is seeping back again. I felt so splendid all day."

"I have some aspirin."

"Uhn-uhn," she said, and this acquired negative stood out strangely against her native speech.

He turned away as she started to take off her shoes,

54

and the sound they made toppling to the floor reminded him of very old days.

She lay back, black-skirted, white-bloused, brown-haired, with one pink hand over her eyes.

"How is everything with you?" asked Pnin (have her say what she wants of me, quick!) as he sank into the white rocker near the radiator.

"Our work is very interesting," she said, still shielding her eyes, "but I must tell you I don't love Eric any more. Our relations have disintegrated. Incidentally Eric dislikes his child. He says he is the land father and you, Timofey, are the water father."

Pnin started to laugh: he rolled with laughter, the rather juvenile rocker fairly cracking under him. His eyes were like stars and quite wet.

She looked at him curiously for an instant from under her plump hand—and went on:

"Eric is one hard emotional block in his attitude toward Victor. I don't know how many times the boy must have killed him in his dreams. And, with Eric, verbalization—I have long noticed—confuses problems instead of clarifying them. He is a very difficult person. What is your salary, Timofey?"

He told her.

"Well," she said, "it is not grand. But I suppose you can even lay something aside—it is more than enough for your needs, for your microscopic needs, Timofey."

Her abdomen tightly girdled under the black skirt jumped up two or three times with mute, cozy, good-natured reminiscential irony—and Pnin blew his nose, shaking his head the while, in voluptuous, rapturous mirth.

"Listen to my latest poem," she said, her hands now

55

along her sides as she lay perfectly straight on her back, and she sang out rhythmically, in long-drawn, deep-voiced tones:

> *"Ya nadela tyomnoe plat'e,*
> *I monashenki ya skromney;*
> *Iz slonovoy kosti raspyat'e*
> *Nad holodnoy postel'yu moey.*
>
> *No ogni nebïvalïh orgiy*
> *Prozhigayut moyo zabïtyo*
> *I shepchi ya imya Georgiy—*
> *Zolotoe imya tvoyo!*
>
> *(I have put on a dark dress*
> *And am more modest than a nun;*
> *An ivory crucifix*
> *Is over my cold bed.*
>
> *But the lights of fabulous orgies*
> *Burn through my oblivion,*
> *And I whisper the name George—*
> *Your golden name!)"*

"He is a very interesting man," she went on, without any interval. "Practically English, in fact. He flew a bomber in the war and now he is with a firm of brokers who have no sympathy with him and do not understand him. He comes from an ancient family. His father was a dreamer, had a floating casino, you know, and all that, but was ruined by some Jewish gangsters in Florida and voluntarily went to prison for another man; it is a family of heroes."

She paused. The silence in the little room was punctuated rather than broken by the throbbing and tinkling in those whitewashed organ pipes.

"I made Eric a complete report," Liza continued with a sigh. "And now he keeps assuring me he can cure me if I co-operate. Unfortunately I am also co-operating with George."

She pronounced George as in Russian—both g's hard, both e's longish.

"Well, *c'est la vie*, as Eric so originally says. How can you sleep with that string of cobweb hanging from the ceiling?" She looked at her wrist watch. "Goodness, I must catch the bus at four-thirty. You must call a taxi in a minute. I have something to say to you of the utmost importance."

Here it was coming at last—so late.

She wanted Timofey to lay aside every month a little money for the boy—because she could not ask Bernard Maywood now—and she might die—and Eric did not care what happened—and somebody ought to send the lad a small sum now and then, as if coming from his mother—pocket money, you know—he would be among rich boys. She would write Timofey giving him an address and some more details. Yes—she never doubted that Timofey was a darling (*"Nu kakoy zhe ti dushka"*). And now where was the bathroom? And would he please telephone for the taxi?

"Incidentally," she said, as he was helping her into her coat and as usual searching with a frown for the fugitive armhole while she pawed and groped, "you know, Timofey, this brown suit of yours is a mistake: a gentleman does not wear brown."

He saw her off, and walked back through the park. To hold her, to keep her—just as she was—with her cruelty, with her vulgarity, with her blinding blue eyes, with her miserable poetry, with her fat feet, with her impure, dry, sordid, infantile soul. All of a sudden he thought: If people are reunited in Heaven (I don't believe it, but suppose), then how shall I stop it from creeping upon me, over me, that shriveled, helpless, lame thing, her soul? But this is the earth, and I am, curiously enough, alive, and there is something in me and in life——

He seemed to be quite unexpectedly (for human despair seldom leads to great truths) on the verge of a simple solution of the universe but was interrupted by an urgent request. A squirrel under a tree had seen Pnin on the path. In one sinuous tendril-like movement, the intelligent animal climbed up to the brim of a drinking fountain and, as Pnin approached, thrust its oval face toward him with a rather coarse spluttering sound, its cheeks puffed out. Pnin understood and after some fumbling he found what had to be pressed for the necessary results. Eying him with contempt, the thirsty rodent forthwith began to sample the stocky sparkling pillar of water, and went on drinking for a considerable time. "She has fever, perhaps," thought Pnin, weeping quietly and freely, and all the time politely pressing the contraption down while trying not to meet the unpleasant eye fixed upon him. Its thirst quenched, the squirrel departed without the least sign of gratitude.

The water father continued upon his way, came to the end of the path, then turned into a side street where there was a small bar of log-cabin design with garnet glass in its casement windows.

When Joan with a bagful of provisions, two magazines, and three parcels, came home at a quarter past five, she found in the porch mailbox a special-delivery air-mail letter from her daughter. More than three weeks had elapsed since Isabel had briefly written her parents to say that, after a honeymoon in Arizona, she had safely reached her husband's home town. Juggling with her packages, Joan tore the envelope open. It was an ecstatically happy letter, and she gulped it down, everything swimming a little in the radiance of her relief. On the outside of the front door she felt, then saw with brief surprise, Pnin's keys, like a bit of his fondest viscera, dangling with their leathern case from the lock; she used them to open the door, and as soon as she had entered she heard, coming from the pantry, a loud anarchistic knocking—cupboards being opened and shut one after the other.

She put her bag and parcels down on the sideboard in the kitchen and asked in the direction of the pantry: "What are you looking for, Timofey?"

He came out of there, darkly flushed, wild-eyed, and she was shocked to see that his face was a mess of unwiped tears.

"I search, John, for the viscous and sawdust," he said tragically.

"I am afraid there is no soda," she answered with her lucid Anglo-Saxon restraint. "But there is plenty of whisky in the dining-room cabinet. However, I suggest we both have some nice hot tea instead."

He made the Russian "relinquishing" gesture.

"No, I don't want anything at all," he said, and sat down at the kitchen table with an awful sigh.

She sat down next to him and opened one of the magazines she had bought.

"We are going to look at some pictures, Timofey."

"I do not want, John. You know I do not understand what is advertisement and what is not advertisement."

"You just relax, Timofey, and I'll do the explaining. Oh, look—I like this one. Oh, this is very clever. We have here a combination of two ideas—the Desert Island and the Girl in the Puff. Now, look, Timofey—please"—he reluctantly put on his reading glasses—"this is a desert island with a lone palm, and this is a bit of broken raft, and this is a shipwrecked mariner, and this is the ship's cat he saved, and this here, on that rock——"

"Impossible," said Pnin. "So small island, moreover with palm, cannot exist in such big sea."

"Well, it exists here."

"Impossible isolation," said Pnin.

"Yes, but—— Really, you are not playing fair, Timofey. You know perfectly well you agree with Lore that the world of the mind is based on a compromise with logic."

"I have reservations," said Pnin. "First of all, logic herself——"

"All right, I'm afraid we are wandering away from our little joke. Now, you look at the picture. So this is the mariner, and this is the pussy, and this is a rather wistful mermaid hanging around, and now look at the puffs right above the sailor and the pussy."

"Atomic bomb explosion," said Pnin sadly.

"No, not at all. It is something much funnier. You see,

60

these round puffs are supposed to be the projections of their thoughts. And now at last we are getting to the amusing part. The sailor imagines the mermaid as having a pair of legs, and the cat imagines her as all fish."

"Lermontov," said Pnin, lifting two fingers, "has expressed everything about mermaids in only two poems. I cannot understand American humor even when I am happy, and I must say——" He removed his glasses with trembling hands, elbowed the magazine aside, and, resting his head on his arm, broke into muffled sobs.

She heard the front door open and close, and a moment later Laurence peeped into the kitchen with facetious furtiveness. Joan's right hand waved him away; her left directed him to the rainbow-rimmed envelope on top of the parcels. The private smile she flashed was a summary of Isabel's letter; he grabbed it and, no more in jest, tiptoed out again.

Pnin's unnecessarily robust shoulders continued to shake. She closed the magazine and for a minute studied its cover: toy-bright school tots, Isabel and the Hagen child, shade trees still off duty, a white spire, the Waindell bells.

"Doesn't she want to come back?" asked Joan softly.

Pnin, his head on his arm, started to beat the table with his loosely clenched fist.

"I haf nofing," wailed Pnin between loud, damp sniffs, "I haf nofing left, nofing, nofing!"

Chapter Three

1

During the eight years Pnin had taught at Waindell College he had changed his lodgings—for one reason or another, mainly sonic—about every semester. The accumulation of consecutive rooms in his memory now resembled those displays of grouped elbow chairs on show, and beds, and lamps, and inglenooks which, ignoring all space-time distinctions, commingle in the soft light of a furniture store beyond which it snows, and the dusk deepens, and nobody really loves anybody. The rooms of his Waindell period looked especially trim in comparison with one he had had in uptown New York, midway between Tsentral Park and Reeverside, on a block memorable for the wastepaper along the curb, the bright pat of dog dirt somebody had already slipped upon, and a tireless boy pitching a ball against the steps of the high brown porch; and even that room became positively dapper in Pnin's mind (where a small ball still rebounded) when compared with the old, now dust-blurred lodgings of his long Central-European, Nansen-passport period.

With age, however, Pnin had become choosy. Pretty fixtures no longer sufficed. Waindell was a quiet townlet, and Waindellville, in a notch of the hills, was yet quieter; but nothing was quiet enough for Pnin. There had been, at the start of his life here, that studio in the thoughtfully furnished College Home for Single Instructors, a very nice place despite certain gregarious drawbacks ("Ping-pong, Pnin?" "I don't any more play at games of infants"), until workmen came and started to drill holes in the street—Brainpan Street, Pningrad—and patch them up again, and this went on and on, in fits of shivering black zigzags and stunned pauses, for weeks, and it did not seem likely they would ever find again the precious tool they had entombed by mistake. There had been (to pick out here and there only special offenders) that room in the eminently hermetic-looking Duke's Lodge, Waindellville: a delightful *kabinet*, above which, however, every evening, among crashing bathroom cascades and banging doors, two monstrous statues on primitive legs of stone would grimly tramp—shapes hard to reconcile with the slender build of his actual upstairs neighbors, who turned out to be the Starrs, of the Fine Arts Department ("I am Christopher, and this is Louise"), an angelically gentle couple keenly interested in Dostoevski and Shostakovich. There had

63

been—in yet another rooming house—a still cozier bedroom-study, with nobody butting in for a free lesson in Russian; but as soon as the formidable Waindell winter began to penetrate the coziness by means of sharp little drafts, coming not only from the window but even from the closet and the base plugs, the room had developed something like a streak of madness or mystic delusion—namely, a tenacious murmur of music, more or less classical, oddly located in Pnin's silver-washed radiator. He tried to muffle it up with a blanket, as if it were a caged songbird, but the song persisted until Mrs. Thayer's old mother was removed to the hospital where she died, upon which the radiator switched to Canadian French.

He tried habitats of another type: rooms for rent in private houses which, although differing from each other in many respects (not all, for instance, were clapboard ones; a few were stucco, or at least partly stucco), had one generic characteristic in common: in their parlor or stair-landing bookcases Hendrik Willem van Loon and Dr. Cronin were inevitably present; they might be separated by a flock of magazines, or by some glazed and buxom historical romance, or even by Mrs. Garnett impersonating somebody (and in such houses there would be sure to hang somewhere a Toulouse-Lautrec poster), but you found the pair without fail, exchanging looks of tender recognition, like two old friends at a crowded party.

2

He had returned for a spell to the College Home, but so had the pavement drillers, and there had cropped up other nuisances besides. At present Pnin was still renting the pink-walled, white-flounced second-floor bedroom in the Clements' house, and this was the first house he really liked and the first room he had occupied for more than a year. By now he had weeded out all trace of its former occupant; or so he thought, for he did not notice, and probably never would, a funny face scrawled on the wall just behind the headboard of the bed and some half-erased height-level marks penciled on the doorjamb, beginning from a four-foot altitude in 1940.

For more than a week now, Pnin had had the run of the house: Joan Clements had left by plane for a Western state to visit her married daughter, and a couple of days later, at the very beginning of his spring course in philosophy, Professor Clements, summoned by a telegram, had flown West too.

Our friend had a leisurely breakfast, pleasantly based on the milk that had not been discontinued, and at half-past nine prepared for his usual walk to the campus.

It warmed my heart, the Russian-intelligentski way he had of getting into his overcoat: his inclined head would demonstrate its ideal baldness, and his large, Duchess of Wonderland chin would firmly press against the crossed ends of his green muffler to hold it in place on his chest while, with a jerk of his broad shoulders, he contrived to get into both armholes at once; another heave and the coat was on.

He picked up his *portfel* (briefcase), checked its contents, and walked out.

He was still at a newspaper's throw from his porch when he remembered a book the college library had urgently requested him to return, for the use of another reader. For a moment he struggled with himself; he still needed the volume; but kindly Pnin sympathized too much with the passionate clamor of another(unknown) scholar not to go back for the stout and heavy tome: It was Volume 18—mainly devoted to Tolstoyana—of *Sovetskiy Zolotoy Fond Literaturi* (Soviet Gold Fund of Literature), *Moskva-Leningrad, 1940.*

3

The organs concerned in the production of English speech sounds are the larynx, the velum, the lips, the tongue (that punchinello in the troupe), and, last but not least, the lower jaw; mainly upon its overenergetic and somewhat ruminant motion did Pnin rely when translating in class passages in the Russian grammar or some poem by Pushkin. If his Russian was music, his English was murder. He had enormous difficulty ("dzeefeecooltsee" in Pninian English) with depalatization, never managing to remove the extra Russian moisture from *t*'s and *d*'s before the vowels he so quaintly softened. His explosive "hat" ("I never go in a hat even in winter") differed from the common American pronunciation of "hot" (typical of Waindell townspeople, for example) only by its briefer duration, and thus sounded very much like the German verb *hat* (has). Long *o*'s with him inevitably became short ones: his "no" sounded positively Italian, and this was accentuated by his trick of triplicating the simple negative ("May I give you a lift, Mr. Pnin?" "No-no-no, I have only two paces from here"). He did not possess (nor was he aware of this lack) any long *oo*: all he could muster when called upon to utter "noon" was the lax

vowel of the German *"nun"* ("I have no classes in after-
nun on Tuesday. Today is Tuesday.")

Tuesday—true; but what day of the month, we wonder. Pnin's birthday for instance fell on February 3, by
the Julian calendar into which he had been born in St.
Petersburg in 1898. He never celebrated it nowadays,
partly because, after his departure from Russia, it sidled
by in a Gregorian disguise (thirteen—no, twelve days
late), and partly because during the academic year he
existed mainly on a motuweth frisas basis.

On the chalk-clouded blackboard, which he wittily
called the grayboard, he now wrote a date. In the crook
of his arm he still felt the bulk of *Zol. Fond Lit.* The
date he wrote had nothing to do with the day this was
in Waindell:

December 26, 1829

He carefully drilled in a big white full stop, and
added underneath:

3:03 P.M. St. Petersburg

Dutifully this was taken down by Frank Backman,
Rose Balsamo, Frank Carroll, Irving D. Herz, beautiful,
intelligent Marilyn Hohn, John Mead, Jr., Peter Volkov,
and Allan Bradbury Walsh.

Pnin, rippling with mute mirth, sat down again at his
desk: he had a tale to tell. That line in the absurd Russian grammar, *"Brozhu li ya vdol' ulits shumnïh*
(Whether I wander along noisy streets)," was really the
opening of a famous poem. Although Pnin was supposed in this Elementary Russian class to stick to language exercises (*"Mama, telefon! Brozhu li ya vdol'
ulits shumnïh. Ot Vladivostoka do Vashingtona 5000*

67

mil'."), he took every opportunity to guide his students on literary and historical tours.

In a set of eight tetrametric quatrains Pushkin described the morbid habit he always had—wherever he was, whatever he was doing—of dwelling on thoughts of death and of closely inspecting every passing day as he strove to find in its cryptogram a certain "future anniversary": the day and month that would appear, somewhere, sometime upon his tombstone.

" 'And where will fate send me', imperfective future, 'death,' " declaimed inspired Pnin, throwing his head back and translating with brave literality, " 'in fight, in travel, or in waves? Or will the neighboring dale'— *dolina,* same word, 'valley' we would now say—'accept my refrigerated ashes', *poussière,* 'cold dust' perhaps more correct. 'And though it is indifferent to the insensible body . . .' "

Pnin went on to the end and then, dramatically pointing with the piece of chalk he still held, remarked how carefully Pushkin had noted the day and even the minute of writing down that poem.

"But," exclaimed Pnin in triumph, "he died on a quite, quite different day! He died——" The chair back against which Pnin was vigorously leaning emitted an ominous crack, and the class resolved a pardonable tension in loud young laughter.

(Sometime, somewhere—Petersburg? Prague?—one of the two musical clowns pulled out the piano stool from under the other, who remained, however, playing on, in a seated, though seatless, position, with his rhapsody unimpaired. Where? Circus Busch, Berlin!)

Pnin did not bother to leave the classroom between his dismissed Elementary and the Advanced that was trickling in. The office where *Zol. Fond Lit.* now lay, partly enveloped in Pnin's green muffler, on the filing case, was on another floor, at the end of a resonant passage and next to the faculty lavatory. Till 1950 (this was 1953—how time flies!) he had shared an office in the German Department with Miller, one of the younger instructors, and then was given for his exclusive use Office R, which formerly had been a lumber room but had now been completely renovated. During the spring he had lovingly Pninized it. It had come with two ignoble chairs, a cork bulletin board, a can of floor wax forgotten by the janitor, and a humble pedestal desk of indeterminable wood. He wangled from the Administration a small steel file with an entrancing locking device. Young Miller, under Pnin's direction, embraced and brought over Pnin's part of a sectional bookcase. From old Mrs. McCrystal, in whose white frame house he had spent a mediocre winter (1949–50), Pnin purchased for three dollars a faded, once Turkish rug. With the help of the janitor he screwed onto the side of the desk a pencil sharpener—that highly satisfying, highly philosophical implement that goes ticonderoga-ticonderoga, feeding on the yellow finish and sweet wood, and ends up in a kind of soundlessly spinning ethereal void as we all must. He had other, even more ambitious plans, such as an armchair and a tall lamp. When, after a summer spent teaching in Washington, Pnin returned to his office, an obese dog lay asleep on his rug, and his furniture had been moved to a darker part of the office, so as to make room for a magnificent stainless-steel desk and a swivel chair to match, in which sat writing and smiling to himself the newly imported Austrian scholar, Dr. Bodo von Falternfels; and thenceforth, so far as Pnin was concerned, Office R had gone to seed.

5

At noon, as usual, Pnin washed his hands and head.

He picked up in Office R his overcoat, muffler, book, and brief case. Dr. Falternfels was writing and smiling; his sandwich was half unwrapped; his dog was dead. Pnin walked down the gloomy stairs and through the Museum of Sculpture. Humanities Hall, where, however, Ornithology and Anthropology also lurked, was connected with another brick building, Frieze Hall, which housed the dining rooms and the Faculty Club, by means of a rather rococo openwork gallery: it went up a slope, then turned sharply and wandered down toward a routine smell of potato chips and the sadness of balanced meals. In summer its trellis was alive with quivering flowers; but now through its nakedness an icy wind blew, and someone had placed a found red mitten upon the spout of the dead fountain that stood where one branch of the gallery led to the President's House.

President Poore, a tall, slow, elderly man wearing dark glasses, had started to lose his sight a couple of years before and was now almóst totally blind. With solar regularity, however, he would be led every day by his niece and secretary to Frieze Hall; he came, a figure of antique dignity, moving in his private darkness to an invisible luncheon, and although everybody had long grown accustomed to his tragic entrance, there was in-

variably the shadow of a hush while he was being
steered to his carved chair and while he groped for the
edge of the table; and it was strange to see, directly
behind him on the wall, his stylized likeness in a mauve
double-breasted suit and mahogany shoes, gazing with
radiant magenta eyes at the scrolls handed him by
Richard Wagner, Dostoevski, and Confucius, a group
that Oleg Komarov, of the Fine Arts Department, had
painted a decade ago into Lang's celebrated mural of
1938, which carried all around the dining room a
pageant of historical figures and Waindell faculty members.

Pnin, who wanted to ask his compatriot something,
sat down beside him. This Komarov, a Cossack's son,
was a very short man with a crew cut and a death's-
head's nostrils. He and Serafima, his large, cheerful,
Moscow-born wife, who wore a Tibetan charm on a
long silver chain that hung down to her ample, soft
belly, would throw Russki parties every now and then,
with Russki hors d'oeuvres and guitar music and more
or less phony folk songs—occasions at which shy graduate students would be taught vodka-drinking rites and
other stale Russianisms; and after such feasts, upon
meeting gruff Pnin, Serafima and Oleg (she raising her
eyes to heaven, he covering his with one hand) would
murmur in awed self-gratitude: "*Gospodi, skol'ko mï im
dayom!* (My, what a lot we give them!)"—"them" being
the benighted American people. Only another Russian
could understand the reactionary and Sovietophile
blend presented by the pseudo-colorful Komarovs, for
whom an ideal Russia consisted of the Red Army, an
anointed monarch, collective farms, anthroposophy, the
Russian Church and the Hydro-Electric Dam. Pnin and

Oleg Komarov were usually in a subdued state of war, but meetings were inevitable, and such of their American colleagues as deemed the Komarovs "grand people" and mimicked droll Pnin were sure the painter and Pnin were excellent friends.

It would be hard to say, without applying some very special tests, which of them, Pnin or Komarov, spoke the worse English; probably Pnin; but for reasons of age, general education, and a slightly longer stage of American citizenship, he found it possible to correct Komarov's frequent English interpolations, and Komarov resented this even more than he did Pnin's *antikvarnïy liberalizm.*

"Look here, Komarov (*Poslushayte, Komarov*"—a rather discourteous manner of address)—said Pnin. "I cannot understand who else here might want this book; certainly none of my students; and if it is you, I cannot understand why you should want it anyway."

"I don't," answered Komarov, glancing at the volume. "Not interested," he added in English.

Pnin moved his lips and lower jaw mutely once or twice, wanted to say something, did not, and went on with his salad.

6

This being Tuesday, he could walk over to his favorite haunt immediately after lunch and stay there till dinner time. No gallery connected Waindell College Library with any other buildings, but it was intimately and securely connected with Pnin's heart. He walked past the great bronze figure of the first president of the college, Alpheus Frieze, in sports cap and knickerbockers, holding by its horns the bronze bicycle he was eternally about to mount, judging by the position of his left foot, forever glued to the left pedal. There was snow on the saddle and snow in the absurd basket that recent pranksters had attached to the handle bars. "*Huligani*," fumed Pnin, shaking his head—and slipped slightly on a flag of the path that meandered down a turfy slope among the leafless elms. Besides the big book under his right arm, he carried in his left hand his brief case, an old, Central European-looking, black *portfel'*, and this he swung rhythmically by its leathern grip as he marched to his books, to his scriptorium in the stacks, to his paradise of Russian lore.

An elliptic flock of pigeons, in circular volitation, soaring gray, flapping white, and then gray again, wheeled across the limpid, pale sky, above the College Library. A train whistled afar as mournfully as in the steppes. A skimpy squirrel dashed over a patch of sunlit snow, where a tree trunk's shadow, olive-green on the turf, became grayish blue for a stretch, while the tree itself, with a brisk, scrabbly sound, ascended, naked, into the sky, where the pigeons swept by for a third and last time. The squirrel, invisible now in a crotch, chattered, scolding the delinquents who would pot him out of his tree. Pnin, on the dirty black ice of the flagged path, slipped again, threw up one arm in an abrupt convulsion, regained his balance, and, with a solitary smile, stooped to pick up *Zol. Fond Ltt.*, which lay wide open to a snapshot of a Russian pasture with Lyov Tolstoy trudging across it toward the camera and some long-maned horses behind him, their innocent heads turned toward the photographer too.

V boyu li, v stranstvii, v volnah? In fight, in travel, or in waves? Or on the Waindell campus? Gently

73

champing his dentures, which retained a sticky layer of cottage cheese, Pnin went up the slippery library steps.

Like so many aging college people, Pnin had long ceased to notice the existence of students on the campus, in the corridors, in the library—anyhere, in brief, save in functional classroom concentrations. In the beginning, he had been much upset by the sight of some of them, their poor young heads on their forearms, fast asleep among the ruins of knowledge; but now, except for a girl's comely nape here and there, he saw nobody in the Reading Room.

Mrs. Thayer was at the circulation desk. Her mother and Mrs. Clements' mother had been first cousins.

"How are you today, Professor Pnin?"

"I am very well, Mrs. Fire."

"Laurence and Joan aren't back yet, are they?"

"No. I have brought this book back because I received this card——"

"I wonder if poor Isabel will really get divorced."

"I have not heard. Mrs. Fire, permit me to ask——"

"I suppose we'll have to find you another room, if they bring her back with them."

"Mrs. Fire, permit me to ask something or other. This card which I received yesterday—could you maybe tell me who is the other reader?"

"Let me check."

She checked. The other reader proved to be Timofey Pnin; Volume 18 had been requested by him the Friday before. It was also true that this Volume 18 was already charged to this Pnin, who had had it since Christmas and now stood with his hands upon it, like an ancestral picture of a magistrate.

"It can't be!" cried Pnin. "I requested on Friday Volume 19, year 1947, not 18, year 1940."

"But look—you wrote Volume 18. Anyway, 19 is still being processed. Are you keeping this?"

"Eighteen, 19," muttered Pnin. "There is not great difference! I put the year correctly, *that* is important! Yes, I still need 18—and send to me a more effishant card when 19 available."

Growling a little, he took the unwieldy, abashed book to his favorite alcove and laid it down there, wrapped in his muffler.

They can't read, these women. The year was plainly inscribed.

As usual he marched to the Periodicals Room and there glanced at the news in the latest (Saturday, February 12—and this was Tuesday, O Careless Reader!) issue of the Russian-language daily published, since 1918, by an émigré group in Chicago. As usual, he carefully scanned the advertisements. Dr. Popov, photographed in his new white smock, promised elderly people new vigor and joy. A music corporation listed Russian phonograph records for sale, such as "Broken Life, a Waltz" and "The Song of a Front-Line Chauffeur." A somewhat Gogolian mortician praised his hearses de luxe, which were also available for picnics. Another Gogolian person, in Miami, offered "a two-room apartment for non-drinkers (*dlya trezvih*), among fruit trees and flowers," while in Hammond a room was wistfully being let "in a small quiet family"—and for no special reason the reader suddenly saw, with passionate and ridiculous lucidity, his parents, Dr. Pavel Pnin and Valeria Pnin, he with a medical journal, she with a political review, sitting in two armchairs, facing each other in a small, cheerfully lighted drawing room on Galernaya Street, St. Petersburg, forty years ago.

He also perused the current item in a tremendously long and tedious controversy between three émigré factions. It had started by Faction A's accusing Faction B of inertia and illustrating it by the proverb, "He wishes to climb the fir tree but is afraid to scrape his shins." This had provoked an acid Letter to the Editor from "An Old Optimist," entitled "Fir Trees and Inertia" and beginning: "There is an old American saying 'He who lives in a glass house should not try to kill two birds with one stone.'" In the present issue, there was a two-thousand-word *feuilleton* contributed by a representative of Faction C and headed "On Fir Trees, Glass Houses, and Optimism," and Pnin read this with great interest and sympathy.

He then returned to his carrell for his own research.

He contemplated writing a *Petite Histoire* of Russian culture, in which a choice of Russian Curiosities, Customs, Literary Anecdotes, and so forth would be presented in such a way as to reflect in miniature *la Grande Histoire*—Major Concatenations of Events. He was still at the blissful stage of collecting his material; and many good young people considered it a treat and an honor to see Pnin pull out a catalogue drawer from the comprehensive bosom of a card cabinet and take it, like a big nut, to a secluded corner and there make a quiet mental meal of it, now moving his lips in soundless comment, critical, satisfied, perplexed, and now lifting his rudimentary eyebrows and forgetting them there, left high upon his spacious brow where they remained long after all trace of displeasure or doubt had gone. He was lucky to be at Waindell. Sometime in the nineties the eminent bibliophile and Slavist John Thurston Todd (his bearded bust presided over the drinking fountain), had visited hospitable Russia, and after his death the books he had amassed there quietly chuted into a remote stack. Wearing rubber gloves so as to avoid being stung by the *amerikanski* electricity in the metal of the shelving, Pnin would go to those books and gloat over them: obscure magazines of the Roaring Sixties in marbled boards; century-old historical monographs, their somnolent pages foxed with fungus spots; Russian classics in horrible and pathetic cameo bindings, whose molded profiles of poets reminded dewy-eyed Timofey of his boyhood, when he could idly palpate on the book cover Pushkin's slightly chafed side whisker or Zhukovski's smudgy nose.

Today from Kostromskoy's voluminous work (Moscow, 1855), on Russian myths—a rare book, not to be removed from the library—Pnin, with a not unhappy sigh, started to copy out a passage referring to the old pagan games that were still practiced at the time, throughout the woodlands of the Upper Volga, in the margins of Christian ritual. During a festive week in May— the so-called Green Week which graded into Whitsuntide—peasant maidens would make wreaths of buttercups and frog orchises; then, singing snatches of ancient love chants, they hung these garlands on riverside willows; and on Whitsunday the wreaths were shaken down into the river, where, unwinding, they floated like so many serpents while the maidens floated and chanted among them.

A curious verbal association struck Pnin at this point; he could not catch it by its mermaid tail but made a note on his index card and plunged back into Kostrom-skoy.

When Pnin raised his eyes again, it was dinnertime.

Doffing his spectacles, he rubbed with the knuckles of the hand that held them his naked and tired eyes and, still in thought, fixed his mild gaze on the window above, where, gradually, through his dissolving meditation, there appeared the violet-blue air of dusk, silver-tooled by the reflection of the fluorescent lights of the ceiling, and, among spidery black twigs, a mirrored row of bright book spines.

Before leaving the library, he decided to look up the correct pronunciation of "interested," and discovered that Webster, or at least the battered 1930 edition lying on a table in the Browsing Room, did not place the stress accent on the third syllable, as he did. He sought a list of errata at the back, failed to find one, and, upon closing the elephantine lexicon, realized with a pang that he had immured somewhere in it the index card with notes that he had been holding all this time. Must now search and search through 2500 thin pages, some torn! On hearing his interjection, suave Mr. Case, a lank, pink-faced librarian with sleek white hair and a bow tie, strolled up, took up the colossus by both ends, inverted it, and gave it a slight shake, whereupon it shed a pocket comb, a Christmas card, Pnin's notes, and a gauzy wraith of tissue paper, which descended with infinite listlessness to Pnin's feet and was replaced by Mr. Case on the Great Seals of the United States and Territories.

Pnin pocketed his index card and, while doing so, recalled without any prompting what he had not been able to recall a while ago:

. . . plïla i pela, pela i plïla . . .
. . . she floated and she sang, she sang and floated *. . .*

Of course! Ophelia's death! *Hamlet!* In good old
Andrey Kroneberg's Russian translation, 1844—the joy
of Pnin's youth, and of his father's and grandfather's
young days! And here, as in the Kostromskoy passage,
there is, we recollect, also a willow and also wreaths.
But where to check properly? Alas, *"Gamlet" Vil'yama
Shekspira* had not been acquired by Mr. Todd, was not
represented in Waindell College Library, and whenever you were reduced to look up something in the
English version, you never found this or that beautiful,
noble, sonorous line that you remembered all your life
from Kroneberg's text in Vengerov's splendid edition.
Sad!

It was getting quite dark on the sad campus. Above
the distant, still sadder hills there lingered, under a
cloud bank, a depth of tortoise-shell sky. The heart-
rending lights of Waindellville, throbbing in a fold of
those dusky hills, were putting on their usual magic,
though actually, as Pnin well knew, the place, when
you got there, was merely a row of brick houses, a
service station, a skating rink, a supermarket. As he
walked to the little tavern in Library Lane for a large
portion of Virginia ham and a good bottle of beer,
Pnin suddenly felt very tired. Not only had the *Zol.
Fond* tome become even heavier after its unnecessary
visit to the library, but something that Pnin had half
heard in the course of the day, and had been reluctant
to follow up, now bothered and oppressed him, as does,
in retrospection, a blunder we have made, a piece of

rudeness we have allowed ourselves, or a threat we have chosen to ignore.

Over an unhurried second bottle, Pnin debated with himself his next move or, rather, mediated in a debate between weary-brained Pnin, who had not been sleeping well lately, and an insatiable Pnin, who wished to continue reading at home, as always, till the 2 A.M. freight train moaned its way up the valley. It was decided at last that he would go to bed immediately after attending the program presented by intense Christopher and Louise Starr every second Tuesday at New Hall, rather high-brow music and unusual movie offerings which President Poore, in answer to some absurd criticism last year, had termed "probably the most inspiring and inspired venture in the entire academic community."

ZFL was now asleep in Pnin's lap. To his left sat two Hindu students. At his right there was Professor Hagen's daughter, a hoydenish Drama major. Komarov, thank goodness, was too far behind for his scarcely interesting remarks to carry.

The first part of the program, three ancient movie shorts, bored our friend: that cane, that bowler, that white face, those black, arched eyebrows, those twitchy nostrils meant nothing to him. Whether the incomparable comedian danced in the sun with chapleted nymphs near a waiting cactus, or was a prehistoric man (the supple cane now a supple club), or was glared at by burly Mack Swain at a hectic night club, old-fashioned, humorless Pnin remained indifferent.

"Clown," he snorted to himself. "Even Glupishkin and Max Linder used to be more comical."

The second part of the program consisted of an impressive Soviet documentary film, made in the late forties. It was supposed to contain not a jot of propaganda, to be all sheer art, merrymaking, and the euphoria of proud toil. Handsome, unkempt girls marched in an immemorial Spring Festival with banners bearing snatches of old Russian ballads such as *"Ruki proch ot Korei," "Bas les mains devant la Corée," "La paz vencera a la guerra," "Der Friede besiegt den Krief."* A flying ambulance was shown crossing a snowy range in Tajikistan. Kirghiz actors visited a sanatorium for coal miners among palm trees and staged there a spontaneous performance. In a mountain pasture somewhere in legendary Ossetia, a herdsman reported by portable radio to the local Republic's Ministry of Agriculture on the birth of a lamb. The Moscow Metro shimmered, with its columns and statues, and six would-be travelers seated on three marble benches. A factory worker's family spent a quiet evening at home, all dressed up, in a parlor choked with ornamental plants, under a great silk lampshade. Eight thousand soccer fans watched a match between Torpedo and Dynamo. Eight thousand citizens at Moscow's Electrical Equipment Plant unanimously nominated Stalin candidate from the Stalin Election District of Moscow. The latest Zim passenger model started out with the factory worker's family and a few other people for a picnic in the country. And then——

"I must not, I must not, oh it is idiotical," said Pnin to himself as he felt—unaccountably, ridiculously, humiliatingly—his tear glands discharge their hot, infantine, uncontrollable fluid.

In a haze of sunshine—sunshine projecting in vaporous shafts between the white boles of birches, drenching the pendulous foliage, trembling in eyelets upon the bark, dripping onto the long grass, shining and smoking among the ghosts of racemose bird cherries in scumbled bloom—a Russian wildwood enveloped the rambler. It was traversed by an old forest road with two soft furrows and a continuous traffic of mushrooms and daisies. The rambler still followed in mind that road as he trudged back to his anachronistic lodgings; was again the youth who had walked through those woods with a fat book under his arm; the road emerged into the romantic, free, beloved radiance of a great field unmowed by time (the horses galloping away and tossing their silvery manes among the tall flowers), as drowsiness overcame Pnin, who was now fairly snug in bed with two alarm clocks alongside, one set at 7:30, the other at 8, clicking and clucking on his night table.

Komarov, in a sky-blue shirt, bent over the guitar he was tuning. A birthday party was in progress, and calm Stalin cast with a thud his ballot in the election of governmental pallbearers. In fight, in travel . . . waves or Waindell. . . ."Wonderful!" said Dr. Bodo von Falternfels, raising his head from his writing.

Pnin had all but lapsed into velvety oblivion when some frightful accident happened outside: groaning and clutching at its brow, a statue was making an extravagant fuss over a broken bronze wheel—and then Pnin was awake, and a caravan of lights and of shadowy humps progressed across the window shade. A car door slammed, a car drove off, a key unlocked the brittle, transparent house, three vibrant voices spoke; the house, and the chink under Pnin's door, lit up with a shiver. It was a fever, it was an infection. In fear and helplessness, toothless, nightshirted Pnin heard a suitcase one-leggedly but briskly stomping upstairs, and a pair of young feet tripping up steps so familiar to them, and one could already make out the sound of eager breathing. . . . In fact, the automatic revival of happy homecomings from dismal summer camps would have actually had Isabel kick open—Pnin's—door, had not her mother's warning yelp stopped her in time.

Chapter Four

1

The King, his father, wearing a very white sports shirt
open at the throat and a very black blazer, sat at a
spacious desk whose highly polished surface twinned
his upper half in reverse, making of him a kind of court
card. Ancestral portraits darkened the walls of the vast
paneled room. Otherwise, it was not unlike the headmaster's study at St. Bart's School, on the Atlantic seaboard, some three thousand miles west of the imagined
Palace. A copious spring shower kept lashing at the
french windows, beyond which young greenery, all
eyes, shivered and streamed. Nothing but this sheet of
rain seemed to separate and protect the Palace from

the revolution that for several days had been rocking the city. . . . Actually, Victor's father was a cranky refugee doctor, whom the lad had never much liked and had not seen now for almost two years.

The King, his more plausible father, had decided not to abdicate. No newspapers were coming out. The Orient Express was stranded, with all its transient passengers, at a suburban station, on the platform of which, reflected in puddles, picturesque peasants stood and gaped at the curtained windows of the long, mysterious cars. The Palace, and its terraced gardens, and the city below the palatial hill, and the main city square, where decapitations and folk dances had already started, despite the weather—all this was at the heart of a cross whose arms terminated in Trieste, Graz, Budapest, and Zagreb, as designated in *Rand Mc-Nally's Ready Reference Atlas of the World*. And at the heart of that heart sat the King, pale and calm, and on the whole closely resembling his son as that underformer imagined he would look at forty himself. Pale and calm, a cup of coffee in his hand, his back to the emerald-and-gray window, the King sat listening to a masked messenger, a corpulent old nobleman in a wet cloak, who had managed to make his way through the rebellion and the rain from the besieged Council Hall to the isolated Palace.

"Abdication! One third of the alphabet!" coldly quipped the King, with the trace of an accent. "The answer is no. I prefer the unknown quantity of exile."

Saying this, the King, a widower, glanced at the desk photograph of a beautiful dead woman, at those great blue eyes, that carmine mouth (it was a colored photo, not fit for a king, but no matter). The lilacs, in sudden premature bloom, wildly beat, like shut-out maskers, at the dripping panes. The old messenger bowed and walked backward through the wilderness of the study, wondering secretly whether it would not be wiser for him to leave history alone and make a dash for Vienna where he had some property.... Of course, Victor's mother was not really dead; she had left his everyday father, Dr. Eric Wind (now in South America), and was about to be married in Buffalo to a man named Church.

Victor indulged night after night in these mild fancies, trying to induce sleep in his cold cubicle which was exposed to every noise in the restless dorm. Generally he did not reach that crucial flight episode when the King alone—*solus rex* (as chess problem makers term royal solitude)—paced a beach on the Bohemian Sea, at Tempest Point, where Percival Blake, a cheerful American adventurer, had promised to meet him with a powerful motorboat. Indeed, the very act of postponing that thrilling and soothing episode, the very protraction of its lure, coming as it did on top of the repetitive fancy, formed the main mechanism of its soporific effect.

An Italian film made in Berlin for American consumption, with a wild-eyed youngster in rumpled shorts, pursued through slums and ruins and a brothel or two by a multiple agent; a version of *The Scarlet Pimpernel*, recently staged at St. Martha's, the nearest girls' school; an anonymous Kafkaesque story in a *ci-devant* avant-garde magazine read aloud in class by Mr. Pennant, a melancholy Englishman with a past; and, not least, the residue of various family allusions of long standing to the flight of Russian intellectuals from

Lenin's regime thirty-five years ago—these were the obvious sources of Victor's fantasies; they may have been, at one time, intensely affecting; by now they had become frankly utilitarian, as a simple and pleasant drug.

2

He was now fourteen but looked two or three years older—not because of his lanky height, close on six feet, but because of a casual ease of demeanor, an expression of amiable aloofness about his plain but clean-cut features, and a complete lack of clumsiness or constraint which, far from precluding modesty and reserve, lent a sunny something to his shyness and a detached blandness to his quiet ways. Under his left eye a brown mole almost the size of a cent punctuated the pallor of his cheek. I do not think he loved anybody.

In his attitude toward his mother, passionate childhood affection had long since been replaced by tender condescension, and all he permitted himself was an inward sigh of amused submission to fate when, in her fluent and flashy New York English, with brash metallic nasalities and soft lapses into furry Russianisms, she regaled strangers in his presence with stories that he had heard countless times and that were either over-embroidered or untrue. It was more trying when among such strangers Dr. Eric Wind, a completely humorless pedant who believed that his English (acquired in a German high school) was impeccably pure, would mouth a stale facetious phrase, saying "the pond" for the ocean, with the confidential and arch air of one who makes his audience the precious gift of a fruity colloquialism. Both parents, in their capacity of psychotherapists, did their best to impersonate Laius and Jocasta, but the boy proved to be a very mediocre little Oedipus. In order not to complicate the modish triangle of Freudian romance (father, mother, child), Liza's first husband had never been mentioned. Only when the Wind marriage started to disintegrate, about the time that Victor was enrolled at St. Bart's, Liza informed him that she had been Mrs. Pnin before she left Europe. She told him that this former husband of hers had migrated to America too—that in fact he would soon see Victor; and since everything Liza alluded to (opening wide her radiant black-lashed blue eyes) invariably took on a veneer of mystery and glamour, the figure of the great Timofey Pnin, scholar and gentleman, teaching a practically dead language at the famous Waindell College some three hundred miles northwest of St. Bart's, acquired in Victor's hospitable mind a curious charm, a family resemblance to those Bulgarian kings or Mediterranean princes who used to be world-famous experts in butterflies or sea shells. He therefore experienced pleasure when Professor Pnin entered into a staid and decorous correspondence with him; a first letter, couched in beautiful French but very indifferently typed, was followed by a picture postcard representing the Gray Squirrel. The card belonged to an educational series depicting Our Mammals and Birds; Pnin had acquired the whole series specially for the purpose of this correspondence. Victor was glad to learn that "squirrel" came from a Greek word which meant "shadow-tail." Pnin invited Victor to visit him during the next vacation and informed the boy that he would meet him at the Waindell bus station. "To be recognized," he wrote, in English, "I will appear in dark spectacles and hold a black brief case with my monogram in silver."

3

Both Eric and Liza Wind were morbidly concerned with heredity, and instead of delighting in Victor's artistic genius, they used to worry gloomily about its genetic cause. Art and science had been represented rather vividly in the ancestral past. Should one trace Victor's passion for pigments back to Hans Andersen (no relation to the bedside Dane), who had been a stained-glass artist in Lübeck before losing his mind (and believing himself to be a cathedral) soon after his beloved daughter married a gray-haired Hamburg jeweler, author of a monograph on sapphires and Eric's maternal grandfather? Or was Victor's almost pathological precision of pencil and pen a by-product of Bogolepov's science? For Victor's mother's great-grandfather, the seventh son of a country pope, had been no other than that singular genius, Feofilakt Bogolepov, whose only rival for the title of greatest Russian mathematician was Nikolay Lobachevski. One wonders.

Genius is non-conformity. At two, Victor did not make little spiral scribbles to express buttons or portholes, as a million tots do, why not you? Lovingly he made his circles perfectly round and perfectly closed. A three-year-old child, when asked to copy a square, shapes one recognizable corner and then is content to render the rest of the outline as wavy or circular; but Victor at three not only copied the researcher's (Dr. Liza Wind's) far from ideal square with contemptuous accuracy but added a smaller one beside the copy. He never went through that initial stage of graphic activity when infants draw *Kopffüsslers* (tadpole people), or humpty dumpties with L-like legs, and arms ending in rake prongs; in fact, he avoided the human form altogether and when pressed by Papa (Dr. Eric Wind) to draw Mama (Dr. Liza Wind), responded with a lovely undulation, which he said was her shadow on the new refrigerator. At four, he evolved an individual stipple. At five, he began to draw objects in perspective —a side wall nicely foreshortened, a tree dwarfed by distance, one object half masking another. And at six, Victor already distinguished what so many adults never learn to see—the colors of shadows, the difference in tint between the shadow of an orange and that of a plum or of an avocado pear.

To the Winds, Victor was a problem child insofar as he refused to be one. From the Wind point of view, every male child had an ardent desire to castrate his father and a nostalgic urge to re-enter his mother's body. But Victor did not reveal any behavior disorder, did not pick his nose, did not suck his thumb, was not even a nail biter. Dr. Wind, with the object of eliminating what he, a radiophile, termed "the static of personal relationship," had his impregnable child tested psychometrically at the Institute by a couple of outsiders, young Dr. Stern and his smiling wife (I am Louis and this is Christina). But the results were either monstrous or nil: the seven-year-old subject scored on the so-called Godunov Drawing-of-an-Animal Test a sensational mental age of seventeen, but on being given a Fairview Adult Test promptly sank to the mentality of a two-year-old. How much care, skill, inventiveness have gone to devise those marvelous techniques! What a shame that certain patients refuse to co-operate! There is, for instance, the Kent-Rosanoff Absolutely Free Association Test, in which little Joe or Jane is asked to respond to a Stimulus Word, such as table, duck, music, sickness, thickness, low, deep, long, happiness, fruit, mother, mushroom. There is the charming Bièvre Interest-Attitude Game (a blessing on rainy afternoons), in which little Sam or Ruby is asked to put a little mark in front of the things about which he or she feels sort of fearful, such as dying, falling, dreaming, cyclones, funerals, father, night, operation, bedroom, bathroom, converge, and so forth; there is the Augusta Angst Abstract Test in which the little one (*das Kleine*) is made to express a list of terms ("groaning," "pleasure," "darkness") by means of unlifted lines. And there is, of course, the Doll Play, in which Patrick or Patricia is given two identical rubber dolls and a cute little bit of clay which Pat must fix on one of them before he or she starts playing, and oh the lovely doll house, with so many rooms and lots of quaint miniature objects, including a chamber pot no bigger than a cupule, and a medicine chest, and a poker, and a double bed, and even a pair of teeny-weeny rubber gloves in the kitchen, and you may be as mean as you like and do anything you want to Papa doll if you think he is beating Mama doll when they put out the lights in the bedroom. But bad Victor would not play with Lou and Tina, ignored the dolls, struck out all the listed words (which was against the rules), and made drawings that had no subhuman significance whatever.

Nothing of the slightest interest to therapists could Victor be made to discover in those beautiful, *beautiful* Rorschach ink blots, wherein children see, or should see, all kinds of things, seascapes, escapes, capes, the worms of imbecility, neurotic tree trunks, erotic galoshes, umbrellas, and dumbbells. Nor did any of Victor's casual sketches represent the so-called mandala—a term supposedly meaning (in Sanskrit) a magic ring, and applied by Dr. Jung and others to any doodle in the shape of a more or less fourfold spreading structure, such as a halved mangosteen, or a cross, or the wheel on which egos are broken like Morphos, or more exactly, the molecule of carbon, with its four valences—that main chemical component of the brain, automatically magnified and reflected on paper.

The Sterns reported that "unfortunately the psychic value of Victor's Mind Pictures and Word Associations is completely obscured by the boy's artistic inclinations." And thenceforth the Winds' little patient, who had trouble in going to sleep and lacked appetite, was allowed to read in bed till after midnight and evade oatmeal in the morning.

4

In planning her boy's education, Liza had been torn between two libidos: to endow him with the latest benefits of Modern Child Psychotherapy, and to find, among American frames of religious reference, the nearest approach to the melodious and wholesome amenities of the Greek Catholic Church, that mild communion whose demands on one's conscience are so small in comparison with the comforts it offers.

Little Victor at first went to a progressive kindergarten in New Jersey, and then, upon the advice of some Russian friends, attended a day school there. The school was directed by an Episcopal clergyman who proved to be a wise and gifted educator, sympathetic to superior children, no matter how bizarre or rowdy they might be; Victor was certainly a little peculiar, but on the other hand very quiet. At twelve, he went to St. Bartholomew's.

Physically, St. Bart's was a great mass of self-conscious red brick, erected in 1869 on the outskirts of Cranton, Massachusetts. Its main building formed three sides of a large quadrangle, the fourth being a cloistered passage. Its gabled gatehouse was glossily coated on one side with American ivy and tipped somewhat top-heavily with a Celtic cross of stone. The ivy rippled in the wind like the back skin of a horse. The hue of red brick is fondly supposed to grow richer with time; that of good old St. Bart's had only grown dirty. Under the cross and immediately over the sonorous-looking but really echoless arc of the entrance was carved a dagger of sorts, an attempt to represent the butcher's knife so reproachfully held (in the Vienna Missal) by St. Bartholomew, one of the Apostles— the one, namely, who had been flayed alive and exposed to the flies in the summer of 65 A.D. or thereabouts, in Albanopolis, now Derbent, southeastern Russia. His coffin, when cast by a furious king into the Caspian Sea, had blandly sailed all the way to Lipari Island off the coast of Sicily—probably a legend, seeing that the Caspian had been strictly an inland affair ever since the Pleistocene. Beneath this heraldic weapon— which rather resembled a carrot pointing upward—an inscription in burnished church text read: *"Sursum."* Two gentle English shepherd dogs belonging to one of the masters and greatly attached to each other could generally be found drowsing in their private Arcadia on a lawn before the gate.

Liza on her first visit to the school had greatly admired everything about it from the fives courts and the chapel to the plaster casts in the corridors and the photographs of cathedrals in the classrooms. The three lower forms were assigned to dormitories with windowed alcoves; there was a master's room at the end. Visitors could not help admiring the fine gymnasium. Very evocative, too, were the oaken seats and hammer-beamed roof of the chapel, a Romanesque structure that had been donated half a century ago by Julius Schonberg, wool manufacturer, brother of the world-famous Egyptologist Samuel Schonberg who perished in the Messina earthquake. There were twenty-five masters and the headmaster, the Reverend Archibald Hopper, who on warm days wore elegant clerical gray and performed his duties in radiant ignorance of the intrigue that was on the point of dislodging him.

5

Although Victor's eye was his supreme organ, it was rather by smells and sounds that the neutral notion of St. Bart's impressed itself on his consciousness. There was the musty, dull reek of old varnished wood in the dorms, and the night sounds in the alcoves—loud gastric explosions and a special squeaking of bed springs, accentuated for effect—and the bell in the hallway, in the hollow of one's headache, at 6:45 A.M. There was the odor of idolatry and incense coming from the burner that hung on chains and on shadows of chains from the ribbed ceiling of the chapel; and there was the Reverend Hopper's mellow voice, nicely blending vulgarity with refinement; and Hymn 166, "Sun of My Soul," which new boys were required to learn by heart; and there was, in the locker room, the immemorial sweat of the hamper on wheels, which held a communal supply of athletic supporters—a beastly gray tangle, from which one had to untwist a strap for oneself to put on at the start of the sport period—and how harsh and sad the clusters of cries from each of the four playing fields!

With an intelligence quotient of about a hundred and eighty and an average grade of ninety, Victor easily ranked first in a class of thirty-six and was, in fact, one of the three best scholars in the school. He had little respect for most of his teachers; but he revered Lake, a tremendously obese man with shaggy eyebrows and hairy hands and an attitude of somber embarrassment in the presence of athletic, rosy-cheeked lads (Victor was neither). Lake was enthroned, Buddhalike, in a curiously neat studio that looked more like a reception room in an art gallery than a workshop. Nothing adorned its pale gray walls except two identically framed pictures: a copy of Gertrude Käsebier's photographic masterpiece "Mother and Child" (1897), with the wistful, angelic infant looking up and away (at what?); and a similarly toned reproduction of the head of Christ from Rembrandt's "The Pilgrims of Emmaus," with the same, though slightly less celestial, expression of eyes and mouth.

He had been born in Ohio, had studied in Paris and Rome, had taught in Ecuador and Japan. He was a recognized art expert, and it puzzled people why, during the past ten winters, Lake chose to bury himself

95

at St. Bart's. While endowed with the morose temper of genius, he lacked originality and was aware of that lack; his own paintings always seemed beautifully clever imitations, although one could never quite tell whose manner he mimicked. His profound knowledge of innumerable techniques, his indifference to "schools" and "trends," his detestation of quacks, his conviction that there was no difference whatever between a genteel aquarelle of yesterday and, say, conventional neoplasticism or banal non-objectivism of today, and that nothing but individual talent mattered—these views made of him an unusual teacher. St. Bart's was not particularly pleased either with Lake's methods or with their results, but kept him on because it was fashionable to have at least one distinguished freak on the staff. Among the many exhilarating things Lake taught was that the order of the solar spectrum is not a closed circle but a spiral of tints from cadmium red and oranges through a strontian yellow and a pale paradisal green to cobalt blues and violets, at which point the sequence does not grade into red again but passes into another spiral, which starts with a kind of lavender gray and goes on to Cinderella shades transcending human perception. He taught that there is no such thing as the Ashcan School or the Cache Cache School or the Cancan School. That the work of art created with string, stamps, a Leftist newspaper, and the droppings of doves is based on a series of dreary platitudes. That there is nothing more banal and more bourgeois than paranoia. That Dali is really Norman Rockwell's twin brother kidnaped by gypsies in babyhood. That Van Gogh is second-rate and Picasso supreme, despite his commercial foibles; and that if Degas could immor-

talize a *calèche*, why could not Victor Wind do the
same to a motor car?

One way to do it might be by making the scenery
penetrate the automobile. A polished black sedan was
a good subject, especially if parked at the intersection
of a tree-bordered street and one of those heavyish
spring skies whose bloated gray clouds and amoeba-
shaped blotches of blue seem more physical than the
reticent elms and evasive pavement. Now break the
body of the car into separate curves and panels; then
put it together in terms of reflections. These will be
different for each part: the top will display inverted
trees with blurred branches growing like roots into a
washily photographed sky, with a whalelike building
swimming by—an architectural afterthought; one side
of the hood will be coated with a band of rich celestial
cobalt; a most delicate pattern of black twigs will be
mirrored in the outside surface of the rear window;
and a remarkable desert view, a distended horizon, with
a remote house here and a lone tree there, will stretch
along the bumper. This mimetic and integrative process
Lake called the necessary "naturalization" of man-made
things. In the streets of Cranton, Victor would find a
suitable specimen of car and loiter around it. Suddenly
the sun, half masked but dazzling, would join him. For
the sort of theft Victor was contemplating there could
be no better accomplice. In the chrome plating, in the
glass of a sun-rimmed headlamp, he would see a view
of the street and himself comparable to the microcosmic
version of a room (with a dorsal view of diminutive
people) in that very special and very magical small
convex mirror that, half a millenium ago, Van Eyck and
Petrus Christus and Memling used to paint into their

97

detailed interiors, behind the sour merchant or the domestic Madonna.

To the latest issue of the school magazine Victor had contributed a poem about painters, over the *nom de guerre* Moinet, and under the motto "Bad reds should all be avoided; even if carefully manufactured, they are still bad" (quoted from an old book on the technique of painting but smacking of a political aphorism). The poem began:

> Leonardo! Strange diseases
> strike at madders mixed with lead:
> nun-pale now are Mona Lisa's
> lips that you had made so red.

He dreamed of mellowing his pigments as the Old Masters had done—with honey, fig juice, poppy oil, and the slime of pink snails. He loved water colors and he loved oils, but was wary of the too fragile pastel and the too coarse distemper. He studied his mediums with the care and patience of an insatiable child—one of those painter's apprentices (it is now Lake who is dreaming!), lads with bobbed hair and bright eyes who would spend years grinding colors in the workshop of some great Italian skiagrapher, in a world of amber and paradisal glazes. At eight, he had once told his mother that he wanted to paint air. At nine, he had known the sensuous delight of a graded wash. What did it matter to him that gentle chiaroscuro, offspring of veiled values and translucent undertones, had long since died behind the prison bars of abstract art, in the poorhouse of hideous primitivism? He placed various objects in turn—an apple, a pencil, a chess pawn, a comb—behind a glass of water and peered through it at each studiously: the red apple became a clear-cut red band bounded by a straight horizon, half a glass of Red Sea, Arabia Felix. The short pencil, if held obliquely, curved like a stylized snake, but if held vertically became monstrously fat—almost pyramidal. The black pawn, if moved to and fro, divided into a couple of black ants. The comb, stood on end, resulted in the glass's seeming to fill with beautifully striped liquid, a zebra cocktail.

6

On the eve of the day on which Victor had planned to arrive, Pnin entered a sport shop in Waindell's Main Street and asked for a football. The request was unseasonable but he was offered one.

"No, no," said Pnin, "I do not wish an egg or, for example, a torpedo. I want a simple football ball. Round!"

And with wrists and palms he outlined a portable world. It was the same gesture he used in class when speaking of the "harmonical wholeness" of Pushkin.

The salesman lifted a finger and silently fetched a soccer ball.

"Yes, this I will buy," said Pnin with dignified satisfaction.

Carrying his purchase, wrapped in brown paper and Scotch-taped, he entered a bookstore and asked for *Martin Eden.*

"Eden, Eden, Eden," the tall dark lady in charge repeated rapidly, rubbing her forehead. "Let me see, you don't mean a book on the British statesman? Or do you?"

"I mean," said Pnin, "a celebrated work by the celebrated American writer Jack London."

"London, London, London," said the woman, holding her temples.

Pipe in hand, her husband, a Mr. Tweed, who wrote topical poetry, came to the rescue. After some search he brought from the dusty depths of his not very prosperous store an old edition of *The Son of the Wolf*.

"I'm afraid," he said, "that's all we have by this author."

"Strange!" said Pnin. "The vicissitudes of celebrity! In Russia, I remember, everybody—little children, full-grown people, doctors, advocates—everybody read and reread him. This is not his best book but O.K., O.K., I will take it."

On coming home to the house where he roomed that year, Professor Pnin laid out the ball and the book on the desk of the guest room upstairs. Cocking his head, he surveyed these gifts. The ball did not look nice in its shapeless wrapping; he disrobed it. Now it showed its handsome leather. The room was tidy and cozy. A schoolboy should like that picture of a snowball knocking off a professor's top hat. The bed had just been made by the cleaning woman; old Bill Sheppard, the landlord, had come up from the first floor and had gravely screwed a new bulb into the desk lamp. A warm humid wind pressed through the open window, and one could hear the noise of an exuberant creek that ran below. It was going to rain. Pnin closed the window.

In his own room, on the same floor, he found a note. A laconic wire from Victor had been transmitted by phone: it said that he would be exactly twenty-four hours late.

Victor and five other boys were being held over one
precious day of Easter vacation for smoking cigars in
the attic. Victor, who had a queasy stomach and no
dearth of olefactory phobias (all of which had been
lovingly concealed from the Winds), had not actually
participated in the smoking, beyond a couple of wry
puffs; several times he had dutifully followed to the
forbidden attic two of his best friends—adventurous,
boisterous boys, Tony Brade, Jr., and Lance Boke. You
penetrated there through the trunk room and then up
an iron ladder, which emerged upon a catwalk right
under the roof. Here the fascinating, strangely brittle
skeleton of the building became both visible and tangible, with all its beams and boards, maze of partitions,
sliced shadows, flimsy laths through which the foot
collapsed to a crepitation of plaster dislodged from
unseen ceilings beneath. The labyrinth ended in a small
platform hooded within a recess at the very peak of the
gable, among a motley mess of old comic books and
recent cigar ashes. The ashes were discovered; the boys
confessed. Tony Brade, the grandson of a famous St.
Bart's headmaster, was given permission to leave, for
family reasons; a fond cousin wished to see him before
sailing for Europe. Wisely, Tony begged to be detained
with the rest.

The headmaster in Victor's time was, as I have already said, the Reverend Mr. Hopper, a dark-haired,
fresh-faced pleasant nonentity, greatly admired by Bos-
tonian matrons. As Victor and his fellow culprits were
at dinner with the entire Hopper family, various crystal-
line hints were dropped here and there, especially by

sweet-voiced Mrs. Hopper, an Englishwoman whose aunt had married an earl; the Reverend might relent and the six boys be taken that last evening to a movie in town instead of being sent early to bed. And after dinner, with a kindly wink, she bade them accompany the Reverend, who briskly walked hallward.

Old-fashioned trustees might find it proper to condone the floggings that Hopper had inflicted on special offenders once or twice in the course of his brief and undistinguished career; but what no boy could stomach was the little mean smirk which crooked the headmaster's red lips as he paused on his way to the hall to pick up a neatly folded square of cloth—his cassock and surplice; the station wagon was at the door, and "putting the clinch on the punishment," as the boys expressed it, the false clergyman treated them to a guest performance at Rudbern, twelve miles away, in a cold brick church, before a meager congregation.

8

Theoretically, the simplest way to reach Waindell from Cranton was to get by taxi to Framingham, catch a fast train to Albany, and then a local for a shorter stretch in a northwestern direction; actually, the simplest way was also the most unpractical one. Whether there was some old solemn feud between those railways, or whether both had united to grant a sporting chance to other means of conveyance, the fact remained that no matter how you juggled with timetables, a three-hour wait at Albany between trains was the briefest you could hope to achieve.

There was a bus leaving Albany at 11 A.M. and arriving at Waindell at around 3 P.M. but that meant taking the 6:31 A.M. train from Framingham; Victor felt he could not get up in time; he took, instead, a slightly later and considerably slower train that allowed him to catch at Albany the last bus to Waindell, which deposited him there at half past eight in the evening.

It rained all the way. It was raining when he arrived at the Waindell terminal. Because of a streak of dreaminess and a gentle abstraction in his nature, Victor in any queue was always at its very end. He had long since grown used to this handicap, as one grows used to weak sight or a limp. Stooping a little because of his height, he followed without impatience the passengers that filed out through the bus onto the shining asphalt: two lumpy old ladies in semitransparent raincoats, like potatoes in cellophane; a small boy of seven or eight with a crew cut and a frail, hollowed nape; a many-angled, diffident, elderly cripple, who declined all assistance and came out in parts; three rosy-kneed Waindell coeds in shorts; the small boy's exhausted mother; a number of other passengers; and then—Victor, with a grip in his hand and two magazines under his arm.

In an archway of the bus station a totally bald man with a brownish complexion, wearing dark glasses and carrying a black brief case, was bending in amiable interrogatory welcome over the thin-necked little boy, who, however, kept shaking his head and pointing to his mother, who was waiting for her luggage to emerge from the Greyhound's belly. Shyly and gaily Victor interrupted the *quid pro quo*. The brown-domed gentleman took off his glasses and, unbending himself, looked up, up, up at tall, tall, tall Victor, at his blue

103

eyes and reddish-brown hair. Pnin's well-developed zygomatic muscles raised and rounded his tanned cheeks; his forehead, his nose, and even his large beautiful ears took part in the smile. All in all, it was an extremely satisfactory meeting.

Pnin suggested leaving the luggage and walking one block—if Victor was not afraid of the rain (it was pouring hard, and the asphalt glistened in the darkness, tarnlike, under large, noisy trees). It would be, Pnin conjectured, a treat for the boy to have a late meal in a diner.

"You arrived well? You had no disagreeable adventures?"

"None, sir."

"You are very hungry?"

"No, sir. Not particularly."

"My name is Timofey," said Pnin, as they made themselves comfortable at a window table in the shabby old diner, "Second syllable pronounced as 'muff,' ahksent on last syllable, 'ey' as in 'prey' but a little more protracted. 'Timofey Pavlovich Pnin,' which means 'Timothy the son of Paul.' The pahtronymic has the ahksent on the first syllable and the rest is sloored—Timofey Pahlch. I have a long time debated with myself—let us wipe these knives and these forks—and have concluded that you must call me simply Mr. Tim or, even shorter, Tim, as do some of my extremely sympathetic colleagues. It is—what do you want to eat? Veal cutlet? O.K., I will also eat veal cutlet—it is naturally a concession to America, my new country, wonderful America which sometimes surprises me but always provokes respect. In the beginning I was greatly embarrassed——"

In the beginning Pnin was greatly embarrassed by the

ease with which first names were bandied about in America: after a single party, with an iceberg in a drop of whisky to start and with a lot of whisky in a little tap water to finish, you were supposed to call a gray-templed stranger "Jim," while he called you "Tim" for ever and ever. If you forgot and called him next morning Professor Everett (his real name to you) it was (for him) a horrible insult. In reviewing his Russian friends throughout Europe and the United States, Timofey Pahlch could easily count at least sixty dear people whom he had intimately known since, say, 1920, and whom he never called anything but Vadim Vadimich, Ivan Hristoforovich, or Samuil Izrailevich, as the case might be, and who called him by his name and patronymic with the same effusive sympathy, over a strong warm handshake, whenever they met: "Ah, Timofey Pahlch! *Nu kak?* (Well how?) *A vï, baten'ka, zdorovo postareli* (Well, well, old boy, you certainly don't look any younger)!"

Pnin talked. His talk did not amaze Victor, who had heard many Russians speak English, and he was not bothered by the fact that Pnin pronounced the word "family" as if the first syllable were the French for "woman."

"I speak in French with much more facility than in English," said Pnin, "but you—*vous comprenez le français? Bien? Assez bien? Un peu?*"

"*Très un peu,*" said Victor.

"Regrettable, but nothing to be done. I will now speak to you about sport. The first description of box in Russian literature we find in a poem by Mihail Lermontov, born 1814, killed 1841—easy to remember. The first description of tennis, on the other hand, is found in *Anna Karenina*, Tolstoy's novel, and is related to year 1875. In youth one day, in the Russian countryside, latitude of Labrador, a racket was given to me to play with the family of the Orientalist Gotovtsev, perhaps you have heard. It was, I recollect, a splendid summer day and we played, played, played until all the twelve balls were lost. You also will recollect the past with interest when old.

"Another game," continued Pnin, lavishly sugaring his coffee, "was naturally *kroket*. I was a champion of *kroket*. However, the favorite national recreation was so-called *gorodki*, which means "little towns." One remembers a place in the garden and the wonderful atmosphere of youth: I was strong, I wore an embroidered Russian shirt, nobody plays now such healthy games."

He finished his cutlet and proceeded with the subject:

"One drew," said Pnin, "a big square on the ground, one placed there, like columns, cylindrical pieces of wood, you know, and then from some distance one threw at them a thick stick, very hard, like a boomerang, with a wide, wide development of the arm—excuse me—fortunately it is sugar, not salt."

"I still hear," said Pnin, picking up the sprinkler and shaking his head a little at the surprising persistence of memory, "I still hear the *trakh!*, the crack when one hit the wooden pieces and they jumped in the air. Will you not finish the meat? You do not like it?"

"It's awfully good," said Victor, "but I am not very hungry."

"Oh, you must eat more, much more if you want to be a footballist."

"I'm afraid I don't care much for football. In fact, I hate football. I'm not very good at any game, really."

"You are not a lover of football?" said Pnin, and a look of dismay crept over his large expressive face. He pursed his lips. He opened them—but said nothing. In silence he ate his vanilla ice cream, which contained no vanilla and was not made of cream.

"We will now take your luggage and a taxi," said Pnin.

As soon as they reached the Sheppard house, Pnin ushered Victor into the parlor and rapidly introduced him to his landlord, old Bill Sheppard, formerly superintendent of the college grounds (who was totally deaf and wore a white button in one ear), and to his brother, Bob Sheppard, who had recently come from Buffalo to live with Bill after the latter's wife died. Leaving Victor with them for a minute, Pnin hastily stomped upstairs. The house was a vulnerable construction, and objects in the rooms downstairs reacted with various vibrations to the vigorous footsteps on the upper landing and to the sudden rasp of a window sash in the guest room.

"Now that picture there," deaf Mr. Sheppard was saying, pointing with a didactic finger at a large muddy water color on the wall, "represents the farm where my brother and I used to spend summers fifty years ago. It was painted by my mother's schoolmate, Grace Wells: her son, Charlie Wells, owns that hotel in Waindell-ville—I am sure Dr. Neen has met him—a very very fine man. My late wife was an artist too. I shall show you some works of hers in a moment. Well, that tree there, behind that barn—you can just make it out——"

A terrible clatter and crash came from the stairs: Pnin, on his way down, had lost his footing.

"In the spring of 1905," said Mr. Sheppard, wagging his index at the picture, "under that cottonwood tree——"

He noticed that his brother and Victor had hurried out of the room to the foot of the stairs. Poor Pnin had come down the last steps on his back. He lay supine for a moment, his eyes moving to and fro. He was helped to his feet. No bones were broken.

Pnin smiled and said: "It is like the splendid story of Tolstoy—you must read one day, Victor—about Ivan Ilyich Golovin who fell and got in consequence kidney of the cancer. Victor will now come upstairs with me."

Victor followed, with grip. There was a reproduction of Van Gogh's "La Berceuse" on the landing and Victor, in passing, acknowledged it with a nod of ironic recognition. The guest room was full of the noise of the rain falling on fragrant branches in the framed blackness of the open window. On the desk lay a wrapped-up book and a ten-dollar bill. Victor beamed and bowed to his gruff but kindly host. "Unwrap," said Pnin.

With courteous eagerness, Victor obeyed. Then he sat down on the edge of the bed and, his auburn hair coming down in glossy lanks over his right temple, his striped tie dangling out of the front of his gray jacket, his bulky gray-flanneled knees parted, zestfully opened the book. He intended to praise it—first, because it was a gift, and second, because he believed it to be a translation from Pnin's mother tongue. He remembered there had been at the Psychotherapeutic Institute a Dr. Yakov London from Russia. Rather unfortunately, Victor lit upon a passage about Zarinska, the Yukon Indian Chief's daughter, and lightheartedly mistook her for a Russian maiden. "Her great black eyes were fixed upon her tribesmen in fear and in defiance. So extreme the tension, she had forgotten to breathe . . ."

"I think I'm going to like this," said polite Victor. "Last summer I read *Crime and— —*. A young yawn distended his staunchly smiling mouth. With sympathy, with approval, with heartache Pnin looked at Liza yawning after one of those long happy parties at the Arbenins' or the Polyanskis' in Paris, fifteen, twenty, twenty-five years ago.

"No more reading today," said Pnin. "I know that it is a very exciting book but you will read and read tomorrow. I wish you good night. The bathroom is across the landing."

He shook hands with Victor and marched to his own room.

9

It still rained. All the lights in the Sheppard house were out. The brook in the gully behind the garden, a trembling trickle most of the time, was tonight a loud torrent that tumbled over itself in its avid truckling to gravity, as it carried through corridors of beech and spruce last year's leaves, and some leafless twigs, and a brand-new, unwanted soccer ball that had recently rolled into the water from the sloping lawn after Pnin disposed of it by defenestration. He had fallen asleep at last, despite the discomfort in his back, and in the course of one of those dreams that still haunt Russian fugitives, even when a third of a century has elapsed since their escape from the Bolsheviks, Pnin saw himself fantastically cloaked, fleeing through great pools of ink under a cloud-barred moon from a chimerical palace, and then pacing a desolate strand with his dead friend Ilya Isidorovich Polyanski as they waited for some mysterious deliverance to arrive in a throbbing boat from beyond the hopeless sea. The Sheppard brothers were both awake in their adjacent beds, on their Beautyrest mattresses; the younger listened in the dark to the rain and wondered if after all they should sell the house with its audible roof and wet garden; the elder lay thinking of silence, of a green damp church-yard, of an old farm, of a poplar that years ago light-ning had struck, killing John Head, a dim, distant rela-tion. Victor had, for once, fallen asleep as soon as he put his head under his pillow—a recently evolved method about which Dr. Eric Wind (sitting on a bench, near a fountain, in Quito, Ecuador) would never learn. Around half past one the Sheppards started to snore, the deaf one doing it with a rattle at the end of each ex-halation and many volumes louder than the other, a modest and melancholy wheezer. On the sandy beach where Pnin was still pacing (his worried friend had gone home for a map), there appeared before him a set of approaching footprints, and he awoke with a gasp. His back hurt. It was now past four. The rain had stopped.

Pnin sighed a Russian "okh-okh-okh" sigh, and sought a more comfortable position. Old Bill Sheppard trudged to the downstairs bathroom, brought down the house, then trudged back.

Presently all were asleep again. It was a pity nobody saw the display in the empty street, where the auroral breeze wrinkled a large luminous puddle, making of the telephone wires reflected in it illegible lines of black zigzags.

Chapter Five

1

From the top platform of an old, seldom used lookout tower—a "prospect tower" as it was formerly termed—that stood on a wooded hill eight hundred feet high, called Mount Ettrick, in one of the fairest of New England's fair states, the adventurous summer tourist (Miranda or Mary, Tom or Jim, whose penciled names were almost obliterated on the balustrade) might observe a vast sea of greenery, composed mainly of maple, beech, tacamahac, and pine. Some five miles west, a slender white church steeple marked the spot where nestled the small town of Onkwedo, once famous for its springs. Three miles north, in a riverside clearing at the foot of a grassy knoll, one could distinguish the gables of an ornate house (variously known as Cook's, Cook's Place, Cook's Castle, or The Pines—its initial appellation). Along the south side of Mount Ettrick, a state highway continued east after passing through Onkwedo. Numerous dirt roads and foot trails crisscrossed the timbered plain within the triangle of land limited by the somewhat tortuous hypotenuse of a rural paved road that weaved northeast from Onkwedo to The Pines, the long cathetus of the state highway just mentioned, and the short cathetus of a river spanned by a steel bridge near Mount Ettrick and a wooden one near Cook's.

On a dull warm day in the summer of 1954, Mary or Almira, or, for that matter, Wolfgang von Goethe, whose name had been carved in the balustrade by some old-fashioned wag, might have noticed an automobile that had turned off the highway just before reaching the bridge and was now nosing and poking this way and that in a maze of doubtful roads. It moved warily and unsteadily, and whenever it changed its mind, it would slow down and raise dust behind like a back-kicking dog. At times it might seem, to a less sympathetic soul than our imagined observer, that this pale blue, egg-shaped two-door sedan, of uncertain age and in mediocre condition, was manned by an idiot. Actually its driver was Professor Timofey Pnin, of Waindell College.

Pnin had started taking lessons at the Waindell Driving School early in the year, but "true understanding," as he put it, had come to him only when, a couple of months later, he had been laid up with a sore back and had done nothing but study with deep enjoyment the forty-page *Driver's Manual*, issued by the State Governor in collaboration with another expert, and the article on "Automobile" in the *Encyclopedia Americana*, with illustrations of Transmissions, and Carburetors, and Brakes, and a Member of the Glidden Tour, *circa* 1905, stuck in the mud of a country road among depressing surroundings. Then and only then was the dual nature of his initial inklings transcended at last as he lay on his sickbed, wiggling his toes and shifting phantom gears. During actual lessons with a harsh instructor who cramped his style, issued unnecessary directives in yelps of technical slang, tried to wrestle the wheel from him at corners, and kept irritating a calm, intelligent pupil with expressions of vulgar detraction, Pnin had been totally unable to combine perceptually the car he was driving in his mind and the car he was driving on the road. Now the two fused at last. If he failed the first time he took his driver's-license test, it was mainly because he started an argument with the examiner in an ill-timed effort to prove that nothing could be more humiliating to a rational creature than being required to encourage the development of a base conditional reflex by stopping at a red light when there was not an earthly soul around, heeled or wheeled. He was more circumspect the next time, and passed. An irresistible senior, enrolled in his Russian Language course, Marilyn Hohn, sold him for a hundred dollars her humble old car: she was getting married to the owner of a far grander machine. The trip from Waindell to Onkwedo, with an overnight stop at a tourist home, had been slow and difficult but uneventful. Just before entering Onkwedo, he had pulled up at a gas station and had got out for a breath of country air. An inscrutable white sky hung over a clover field, and from a pile of firewood near a shack came a rooster's cry, jagged and gaudy—a vocal coxcomb. Some chance intonation on the part of this slightly hoarse bird, combined with the warm wind pressing itself against Pnin in search of attention, recognition, anything, briefly reminded him of a dim dead day when he, a Petrograd University freshman, had arrived at the small station of a Baltic summer resort, and the sounds, and the smells, and the sadness——

"Kind of muggy," said the hairy-armed attendant, as he started to wipe the windshield.

Pnin took a letter out of his wallet, unfolded the tiny mimeographed-sketch map attached to it, and asked the attendant how far was the church at which one was supposed to turn left to reach Cook's Place. It was really striking how the man resembled Pnin's colleague at Waindell College, Dr. Hagen—one of those random likenesses as pointless as a bad pun.

"Well, there is a better way to get there," said the false Hagen. "The trucks have messed up that road, and besides you won't like the way it winds. Now you just drive on. Drive through the town. Five miles out of Onkwedo, just after you have passed the trail to Mount Ettrick on your left, and just before reaching the bridge, take the first left turn. It's a good gravel road."

He stepped briskly around the hood and lunged with his rag at the windshield from the other side.

"You turn north and go on bearing north at each crossing—there are quite a few logging trails in those woods but you just bear north and you'll get to Cook's in twelve minutes flat. You can't miss it."

Pnin had now been in that maze of forest roads for about an hour and had come to the conclusion that "bear north," and in fact the word "north" itself, meant

114

nothing to him. He also could not explain what had compelled him, a rational being, to listen to a chance busybody instead of firmly following the pedantically precise instructions that his friend, Alexandr Petrovich Kukolnikov (known locally as Al Cook) had sent him when inviting him to spend the summer at his large and hospitable country house. Our luckless car operator had by now lost himself too thoroughly to be able to go back to the highway, and since he had little experience in maneuvering on rutty narrow roads, with ditches and even ravines gaping on either side, his various indecisions and gropings took those bizarre visual forms that an observer on the lookout tower might have followed with a compassionate eye; but there was no living creature in that forlorn and listless upper region except for an ant who had his own troubles, having, after hours of inept perseverance, somehow reached the upper platform and the balustrade (his *autostrada*) and was getting all bothered and baffled much in the same way as that preposterous toy car progressing below. The wind had subsided. Under the pale sky the sea of tree tops seemed to harbor no life. Presently, however, a gun shot popped, and a twig leaped into the sky. The dense upper boughs in that part of the otherwise stirless forest started to move in a receding sequence of shakes or jumps, with a swinging lilt from tree to tree, after which all was still again. Another minute passed, and then everything happened at once: the ant found an upright beam leading to the roof of the tower and started to ascend it with renewed zest; the sun appeared; and Pnin at the height of hopelessness, found himself on a paved road with a rusty but still glistening sign directing wayfarers "To The Pines."

Al Cook was a son of Piotr Kukolnikov, wealthy Moscow merchant of Old-Believers antecedents, self-made man, Maecenas and philanthropist—the famous Kukolnikov who under the last Tsar had been twice imprisoned in a fairly comfortable fortress for giving financial assistance to Social-Revolutionary groups (terrorists, mainly), and under Lenin had been put to death as an "Imperialistic spy" after almost a week of medieval tortures in a Soviet jail. His family reached America via Harbin, around 1925, and young Cook by dint of quiet perseverance, practical acumen, and some scientific training, rose to a high and secure position in a great chemical concern. A kindly, very reserved man of stocky build, with a large immobile face that was tied up in the middle by a neat little pince-nez, he looked what he was—a Business Executive, a Mason, a Golfer, a prosperious and cautious man. He spoke beautifully correct, neutral English, with only the softest shadow of a Slavic accent, and was a delightful host, of the silent variety, with a twinkling eye, and a highball in each hand; and only when some very old and beloved Russian friend was his midnight guest would Alexandr Petrovich suddenly start to discuss God, Lermontov, Liberty, and divulge a hereditary streak of rash idealism that would have greatly confused a Marxist eavesdropper.

He married Susan Marshall, the attractive, voluble, blond daughter of Charles G. Marshall, the inventor, and because one could not imagine Alexandr and Susan otherwise than raising a huge healthy family, it came as a shock to me and other well-wishers to learn that as the result of an operation Susan would remain childless all her life. They were still young, loved each other with a sort of old-world simplicity and integrity very soothing to observe, and instead of populating their country place with children and grandchildren, they collected, every even-year summer, elderly Russians (Cook's fathers or uncles, as it were); on odd-year summers they would have *amerikantsï* (Americans), Alexandr's business acquaintances or Susan's relatives and friends.

This was the first time Pnin was coming to The Pines but I had been there before. Émigré Russians—liberals and intellectuals who had left Russia around 1920—could be found swarming all over the place. You would find them in every patch of speckled shade, sitting on rustic benches and discussing émigré writers—Bunin, Aldanov, Sirin; lying suspended in hammocks, with the Sunday issue of a Russian-language newspaper over their faces in traditional defense against flies; sipping tea with jam on the veranda; walking in the woods and wondering about the edibility of local toadstools.

Samuil Lvovich Shpolyanski, a large majestically calm old gentleman, and small, excitable, stuttering Count Fyodor Nikitich Poroshin, both of whom, around 1920, had been members of one of those heroic Regional Governments that were formed in the Russian provinces by democratic groups to withstand Bolshevik dictatorship, would pace the avenue of pines and discuss the tactics to be adopted at the next joint meeting of the Free Russia Committee (which they had founded in New York) with another, younger, anti-Communist organization. From a pavilion half smothered by locust trees came fragments of a heated exchange between Professor Bolotov, who taught the History of Philoso-

117

phy, and Professor Chateau, who taught the Philosophy of History: "Reality is Duration," one voice, Bolotov's, would boom. "It is not!" the other would cry. "A soap bubble is as real as a fossil tooth!"

Pnin and Chateau, both born in the late nineties of the nineteenth century, were comparative youngsters. Most of the other men had seen sixty and had trudged on. On the other hand, a few of the ladies, such as Countess Poroshin and Madam Bolotov, were still in their late forties and, thanks to the hygienic atmosphere of the New World, had not only preserved, but improved, their good looks. Some parents brought their offspring with them—healthy, tall, indolent, difficult American children of college age, with no sense of nature, and no Russian, and no interest whatsoever in the niceties of their parents' backgrounds and pasts. They seemed to live at The Pines on a physical and mental plane entirely different from that of their parents: now and then passing from their own level to ours through a kind of interdimensional shimmer; responding curtly to a well-meaning Russian joke or anxious piece of advice, and then fading away again; keeping always aloof (so that one felt one had engendered a brood of elves), and preferring any Onkwedo store product, any sort of canned goods to the marvelous Russian foods provided by the Kukolnikov household at loud, long dinners on the screened porch. With great distress Poroshin would say of his children (Igor and Olga, college sophomores) "My twins are exasperating. When I see them at home during breakfast or dinner and try to tell them most interesting, most exciting things—for instance, about local elective self-government in the Russian Far North in the seventeenth century or, say, something about the history of the first medical schools in Russia—there is, by the way, an excellent monograph by Chistovich on the subject, published in 1883—they simply wander off and turn on the radio in their rooms." Both young people were around the summer Pnin was invited to The Pines. But they stayed invisible; they would have been hideously bored in this out-of-the-way place, had not Olga's admirer, a college boy whose surname nobody seemed to know, arrived from Boston for the weekend in a spectacular car, and had not Igor found a congenial companion in Nina, the Bolotov girl, a handsome slattern with Egyptian eyes and brown limbs, who went to a dancing school in New York.

The household was looked after by Praskovia, a sturdy, sixty-year-old woman of the people with the vivacity of one a score of years younger. It was an exhilarating sight to watch her as she stood on the back porch surveying the chickens, knuckles on hips, dressed in baggy homemade shorts and a matronly blouse with rhinestones. She had nursed Alexandr and his brother when both were children in Harbin and now she was helped in her household duties by her husband, a gloomy and stolid old Cossack whose main passions in life were amateur bookbinding—a self-taught and almost pathological process that he was impelled to inflict upon any old catalogue or pulp magazine that came his way; the making of fruit liqueurs; and the killing of small forest animals.

Of that season's guests, Pnin knew well Professor Chateau, a friend of his youth, with whom he had attended the University of Prague in the early twenties, and he was also well acquainted with the Bolotovs, whom he had last seen in 1949 when he welcomed them

119

with a speech at a formal dinner given them by the Association of Russian Émigré Scholars at the Barbizon-Plaza, upon the occasion of Bolotov's arrival from France. Personally, I never cared much for Bolotov and his philosophical works, which so oddly combine the obscure and the trite; the man's achievement is perhaps a mountain—but a mountain of platitudes; I have always liked, however, Varvara, the seedy philosopher's exuberant buxom wife. When she first visited The Pines, in 1951, she had never seen the New England countryside before. Its birches and bilberries deceived her into placing mentally Lake Onkwedo, not on the parallel of, say, Lake Ohrida in the Balkans, where it belonged, but on that of Lake Onega in northern Russia, where she had spent her first fifteen summers, before fleeing from the Bolsheviks to western Europe, with her aunt Lidia Vinogradov, the well-known feminist and social worker. Consequently the sight of a hummingbird in probing flight, or a catalpa in ample bloom, produced upon Varvara the effect of some unnatural or exotic vision. More fabulous than pictures in a bestiary were to her the tremendous porcupines that came to gnaw at the delicious, gamy old wood of the house, or the elegant, eerie little skunks that sampled the cat's milk in the backyard. She was nonplused and enchanted by the number of plants and creatures she could not identify, mistook Yellow Warblers for stray canaries, and on the occasion of Susan's birthday was known to have brought, with pride and panting enthusiasm, for the ornamentation of the dinner table, a profusion of beautiful poison-ivy leaves, hugged to her pink, freckled breast.

The Bolotovs and Madam Shpolyanski, a little lean woman in slacks, were the first people to see Pnin as he cautiously turned into a sandy avenue, bordered with wild lupines, and, sitting very straight, stiffly clutching the steering wheel as if he were a farmer more used to his tractor than to his car, entered, at ten miles an hour and in first gear, the grove of old, disheveled, curiously authentic-looking pines that separated the paved road from Cook's Castle.

Varvara buoyantly rose from the seat of the pavilion—where she and Roza Shpolyanski had just discovered Bolotov reading a battered book and smoking a forbidden cigarette. She greeted Pnin with a clapping of hands, while her husband showed as much geniality as he was capable of by slowly waving the book he had closed on his thumb to mark the place. Pnin killed the motor and sat beaming at his friends. The collar of his green sport shirt was undone; his partly unzipped windbreaker seemed too tight for his impressive torso; his bronzed bald head, with the puckered brow and conspicuous vermicular vein on the temple, bent low as he wrestled with the door handle and finally dived out of the car.

"*Avtomobil', kostyum—nu pryamo amerikanets* (a veritable American), *pryamo Ayzenhauer!*" said Varvara, and introduced Pnin to Roza Abramovna Shpolyanski.

"We had some mutual friends forty years ago," remarked that lady, peering at Pnin with curiosity.

"Oh, let us not mention such astronomical figures," said Bolotov, approaching and replacing with a grass blade the thumb he had been using as a bookmarker. "You know," he continued, shaking Pnin's hand, "I am rereading *Anna Karenin* for the seventh time and I derive as much rapture as I did, not forty, but sixty, years ago, when I was a lad of seven. And, every time, one discovers new things—for instance I notice now that Lyov Nikolaich does not know on what day his novel starts: it seems to be Friday because that is the day the clockman comes to wind up the clocks in the Oblonski house, but it is also Thursday as mentioned in the conversation at the skating rink between Lyovin and Kitty's mother."

"What on earth does it matter," cried Varvara. "Who on earth wants to know the exact day?"

"I can tell you the exact day," said Pnin, blinking in the broken sunlight and inhaling the remembered tang of northern pines. "The action of the novel starts in the beginning of 1872, namely on Friday, February the twenty-third by the New Style. In his morning paper Oblonski reads that Beust is rumored to have proceeded to Wiesbaden. This is of course Count Friedrich Ferdinand von Beust, who had just been appointed Austrian Ambassador to the Court of St. James's. After presenting his credentials, Beust had gone to the continent for a rather protracted Christmas vacation—had spent there two months with his family, and was now returning to London, where, according to his own memoirs in two volumes, preparations were under way for the thanksgiving service to be held in St. Paul's on February the twenty-seventh for the recovering from typhoid fever of the Prince of Wales. However (*odnako*), it really is hot here (*i zharko zhe u vas*)! I think I shall now present myself before the most luminous orbs (*presvetlïe ochi,* jocular) of Alexandr Petrovich and then go for a dip (*okupnutsya,* also jocular) in the river he so vividly describes in his letter."

"Alexandr Petrovich is away till Monday, on business or pleasure," said Varvara Bolotov, "but I think you will find Susanna Karlovna sun-bathing on her favorite lawn behind the house. Shout before you approach too near."

4

Cook's Castle was a three-story brick-and-timber mansion built around 1860 and partly rebuilt half a century later, when Susan's father purchased it from the Dudley-Greene family in order to make of it a select resort hotel for the richer patrons of the curative Onkwedo Springs. It was an elaborate and ugly building in a mongrel style, with the Gothic bristling through remnants of French and Florentine, and when originally designed might have belonged to the variety which Samuel Sloan, an architect of the time, classified as An Irregular Northern Villa "well adapted to the highest requirements of social life" and called "Northern" because of "the aspiring tendency of its roof and towers." The piquancy of these pinnacles and the merry, somewhat even inebriated air the mansion had of having been composed of several smaller Northern Villas, hoisted into mid-air and knocked together anyhow, with parts of unassimilated roofs, half-hearted gables, cornices, rustic quoins, and other projections sticking out on all sides, had, alas, but briefly attracted tourists. By 1920, the Onkwedo waters had mysteriously lost whatever magic they had contained, and after her father's death Susan had vainly tried to sell The Pines, since they had another more comfortable house in the residential quarter of the industrial city where her husband worked. However, now that they had got accustomed to use the Castle for entertaining their numerous friends, Susan was glad that the meek beloved monster had found no purchaser.

Within, the diversity was as great as without. Four spacious rooms opened from the large hall that retained something of its hostelic stage in the generous dimensions of the grate. The hand rail of the stairs, and at least one of its spindles, dated from 1720, having been transferred to the house, while it was being built, from a far older one, whose very site was no longer exactly known. Very ancient, too, were the beautiful sideboard panels of game and fish in the dining room. In the half a dozen rooms of which each of the upper floors consisted, and in the two wings in the rear, one could discover, among disparate pieces of furniture, some charming satinwood bureau, some romantic rosewood sofa, but also all kinds of bulky and miserable articles, broken chairs, dusty marble-topped tables, morose *étagères* with bits of dark-looking glass in the back as mournful as the eyes of old apes. The chamber Pnin got was a pleasant southeast one on the upper floor: it had remnants of gilt paper on the walls, an army cot, a plain washstand, and all kinds of shelves, brackets, and scrollwork moldings. Pnin shook open the casement, smiled at the smiling forest, again remembered a distant first day in the country, and presently walked down, clad in a new navy-blue bathrobe and wearing on his bare feet a pair of ordinary rubber overshoes, a sensible precaution if one intends to walk through damp and, perhaps, snake-infested grass. On the garden terrace he found Chateau.

Konstantin Ivanich Chateau, a subtle and charming scholar of pure Russian lineage despite his surname (derived, I am told, from that of a Russianized Frenchman who adopted orphaned Ivan), taught at a large New York university and had not seen his very dear Pnin for at least five years. They embraced with a warm rumble of joy. I confess to have been myself, at one time, under the spell of angelic Konstantin Ivanich, namely, when we used to meet every day in the winter of 1935 or 1936 for a morning stroll under the laurels and nettle trees of Grasse, southern France, where he then shared a villa with several other Russian expatriates. His soft voice, the gentlemanly St. Petersburgan burr of his *r*'s, his mild, melancholy caribou eyes, the auburn goatee he continuously twiddled, with a shredding motion of his long, frail fingers—everything about Chateau (to use a literary formula as old-fashioned as he) produced a rare sense of well-being in his friends. Pnin and he talked for a while, comparing notes. As not unusual with firm-principled exiles, every time they met after a separation they not only endeavored to catch up with a personal past, but also to sum up by means of a few rapid passwords—allusions, intonations impossible to render in a foreign language—the course of recent Russian history, thirty-five years of hopeless injustice following a century of struggling justice and glimmering hope. Next, they switched to the usual shop talk of European teachers abroad, sighing and shaking heads over the "typical American college student" who does not know geography, is immune to noise, and thinks education is but a means to get eventually a remunerative job. Then they inquired about each other's work in progress, and both were extremely modest and reticent about their respective researches. Finally, as they walked along a meadow path, brushing against the goldenrod, toward the wood where a rocky river ran, they spoke of their healths: Chateau, who looked so jaunty, with one hand in the pocket of his white flannel trousers and his lustring coat rather rakishly opened on a flannel waistcoat, cheerfully said that in the near future he would have to undergo an exploratory operation of the abdomen, and Pnin said, laughing, that every time *he* was X-rayed, doctors vainly tried to puzzle out what they termed "a shadow behind the heart."

"Good title for a bad novel," remarked Chateau.

As they were passing a grassy knoll just before entering the wood, a pink-faced venerable man in a seersucker suit, with a shock of white hair and a tumefied purple nose resembling a huge raspberry, came striding toward them down the sloping field, a look of disgust contorting his features.

"I have to go back for my hat," he cried dramatically as he drew near.

"Are you acquainted?" murmured Chateau, fluttering his hands introductively. "Timofey Pavlich Pnin, Ivan Ilyich Gramineev."

"*Moyo pochtenie* (My respects)," said both men, bowing to each other over a powerful handshake.

"I thought," resumed Gramineev, a circumstantial narrator, "that the day would continue as overcast as it had begun. By stupidity (*po gluposti*) I came out with an unprotected head. Now the sun is roasting my brains. I have to interrupt my work."

He gestured toward the top of the knoll. There his

easel stood in delicate silhouette against the blue sky. From that crest he had been painting a view of the valley beyond, complete with quaint old barn, gnarled apple tree, and kine.

"I can offer you my panama," said kind Chateau, but Pnin had already produced from his bathrobe pocket a large red handkerchief: he expertly twisted each of its corners into a knot.

"Admirable. . . . Most grateful," said Gramineev, adjusting this headgear.

"One moment," said Pnin. "You must tuck in the knots."

This done, Gramineev started walking up the field toward his easel. He was a well-known, frankly academic painter, whose soulful oils—"Mother Volga," "Three Old Friends" (lad, nag, dog), "April Glade," and so forth—still graced a museum in Moscow.

"Somebody told me," said Chateau, as he and Pnin continued to progress riverward, "that Liza's boy has an extraordinary talent for painting. Is that correct?"

"Yes," answered Pnin. "All the more vexing (*tem bolee obidno*) that his mother, who I think is about to marry a third time, took Victor suddenly to California for the rest of the summer, whereas if he had accompanied me here, as had been planned, he would have had the splendid opportunity of being coached by Gramineev."

"You exaggerate the splendor," softly rejoined Chateau.

They reached the bubbling and glistening stream. A concave ledge between higher and lower diminutive cascades formed a natural swimming pool under the alders and pines. Chateau, a non-bather, made himself comfortable on a boulder. Throughout the academic year Pnin had regularly exposed his body to the radiation of a sun lamp; hence, when he stripped down to his bathing trunks, he glowed in the dappled sunlight of the riverside grove with a rich mahogany tint. He removed his cross and his rubbers.

"Look, how pretty," said observant Chateau.

A score of small butterflies, all of one kind, were settled on a damp patch of sand, their wings erect and closed, showing their pale undersides with dark dots and tiny orange-rimmed peacock spots along the hindwing margins; one of Pnin's shed rubbers disturbed some of them and, revealing the celestial hue of their upper surface, they fluttered around like blue snowflakes before settling again.

"Pity Vladimir Vladimirovich is not here," remarked Chateau. "He would have told us all about these enchanting insects."

"I have always had the impression that his entomology was merely a pose."

"Oh no," said Chateau. "You will lose it some day," he added, pointing to the Greek Catholic cross on a golden chainlet that Pnin had removed from his neck and hung on a twig. Its glint perplexed a cruising dragonfly.

"Perhaps I would not mind losing it," said Pnin. "As you well know, I wear it merely from sentimental reasons. And the sentiment is becoming burdensome. After all, there is too much of the physical about this attempt to keep a particle of one's childhood in contact with one's breastbone."

"You are not the first to reduce faith to a sense of

touch," said Chateau, who was a practicing Greek Catholic and deplored his friend's agnostic attitude.

A horsefly applied itself, blind fool, to Pnin's bald head, and was stunned by a smack of his meaty palm.

From a smaller boulder than the one upon which Chateau was perched, Pnin gingerly stepped down into the brown and blue water. He noticed he still had his wrist watch—removed it and left it inside one of his rubbers. Slowly swinging his tanned shoulders, Pnin waded forth, the loopy shadows of leaves shivering and slipping down his broad back. He stopped and breaking the glitter and shade around him, moistened his inclined head, rubbed his nape with wet hands, soused in turn each armpit, and then, joining both palms, glided into the water, his dignified breast stroke sending off ripples on either side. Around the natural basin, Pnin swam in state. He swam with a rhythmical splutter— half gurgle, half puff. Rhythmically he opened his legs and widened them out at the knees while flexing and straightening out his arms like a giant frog. After two minutes of this, he waded out and sat on the boulder to dry. Then he put on his cross, his wrist watch, his rubbers, and his bathrobe.

5

Dinner was served on the screened porch. As he sat down next to Bolotov and began to stir the sour cream in his red *botvinia* (chilled beet soup), wherein pink ice cubes tinkled, Pnin automatically resumed an earlier conversation.

"You will notice," he said, "that there is a significant difference between Lyovin's spiritual time and Vronski's physical one. In mid-book, Lyovin and Kitty lag behind Vronski and Anna by a whole year. When, on a Sunday evening in May 1876, Anna throws herself under that freight train, she has existed more than four years since the beginning of the novel, but in the case of the Lyovins, during the same period, 1872 to 1876, hardly three years have elapsed. It is the best example of relativity in literature that is known to me."

After dinner, a game of croquet was suggested. These people favored the time-honored but technically illegal setting of hoops, where two of the ten are crossed at the center of the ground to form the so-called Cage or Mousetrap. It became immediately clear that Pnin, who teemed with Madam Bolotov against Shpolyanski and Countess Poroshin, was by far the best player of the lot. As soon as the pegs were driven in and the game started, the man was transfigured. From his habitual, slow, ponderous, rather rigid self, he changed into a terrifically mobile, scampering, mute, sly-visaged hunchback. It seemed to be always his turn to play. Holding his mallet very low and daintily swinging it between his parted spindly legs (he had created a minor sensation by changing into Bermuda shorts expressly for the game), Pnin foreshadowed every stroke with nimble aim-taking oscillations of the mallet head, then gave the ball an accurate tap, and forthwith, still hunched, and with the ball still rolling, walked rapidly to the spot where he had planned for it to stop. With geometrical gusto, he ran it through hoops, evoking cries of admiration from the onlookers. Even Igor Poroshin, who was passing by like a shadow with two cans of beer he was carrying to some private banquet, stopped for a second and shook his head appreciatively before vanishing in the shrubbery. Plaints and protests, however, would mingle with the applause when Pnin, with brutal indifference, croqueted, or rather rocketed, an adversary's ball. Placing in contact with it his own ball, and firmly putting his curiously small foot upon the latter, he would bang at his ball so as to drive the other up the country by the shock of the stroke. When appealed to, Susan said it was completely against the rules, but Madam Shpolyanski insisted it was perfectly acceptable and said that when she was a child her English governess used to call it a Hong Kong.

After Pnin had tolled the stake and all was over, and Varvara accompanied Susan to get the evening tea ready, Pnin quietly retired to a bench under the pines. A certain extremely unpleasant and frightening cardiac sensation, which he had experienced several times throughout his adult life, had come upon him again. It was not pain or palpitation, but rather an awful feeling of sinking and melting into one's physical surroundings —sunset, red boles of trees, sand, still air. Meanwhile Roza Shpolyanski, noticing Pnin sitting alone, and taking advantage of this, walked over to him ("*sidite, sidite!*" don't get up) and sat down next to him on the bench.

"In 1916 or 1917," she said, "you may have had occasion to hear my maiden name—Geller—from some great friends of yours."

"No, I don't recollect," said Pnin.

"It is of no importance, anyway. I don't think we ever met. But you knew well my cousins, Grisha and Mira Belochkin. They constantly spoke of you. He is living in Sweden, I think—and, of course, you have heard of his poor sister's terrible end. . . ."

"Indeed, I have," said Pnin.

"Her husband," said Madam Shpolyanski, "was a most charming man. Samuil Lvovich and I knew him and his first wife, Svetlana Chertok, the pianist, very intimately. He was interned by the Nazis separately from Mira, and died in the same concentration camp as did my elder brother Misha. You did not know Misha, did you? He was also in love with Mira once upon a time."

"*Tshay gotoff* (tea's ready)," called Susan from the porch in her funny functional Russian. "Timofey, Rozochka! *Tshay!*"

Pnin told Madam Shpolyanski he would follow her in a minute, and after she had gone he continued to sit in the first dusk of the arbor, his hands clasped on the croquet mallet he still held.

Two kerosene lamps cozily illuminated the porch of the country house. Dr. Pavel Antonovich Pnin, Timofey's father, an eye specialist, and Dr. Yakov Grigorievich Belochkin, Mira's father, a pediatrician, could not be torn away from their chess game in a corner of the veranda, so Madam Belochkin had the maid serve them there—on a special small Japanese table, near the one they were playing at—their glasses of tea in silver holders, the curd and whey with black bread, the Garden Strawberries, *zemlyanika*, and the other cultivated species, *klubnika* (Hautbois or Green Strawberries), and the radiant golden jams, and the various biscuits, wafers, pretzels, zwiebacks—instead of calling the two engrossed doctors to the main table at the other end of the porch, where sat the rest of the family and guests, some clear, some grading into a luminous mist.

Dr. Belochkin's blind hand took a pretzel; Dr. Pnin's seeing hand took a rook. Dr. Belochkin munched and stared at the hole in his ranks; Dr. Pnin dipped an abstract zwieback into the hole of his tea.

The country house that the Belochkins rented that summer was in the same Baltic resort near which the widow of General N—— let a summer cottage to the Pnins on the confines of her vast estate, marshy and rugged, with dark woods hemming in a desolate manor. Timofey Pnin was again the clumsy, shy, obstinate, eighteen-year-old boy, waiting in the dark for Mira— and despite the fact that logical thought put electric bulbs into the kerosene lamps and reshuffled the people, turning them into aging émigrés and securely, hopelessly, forever wire-netting the lighted porch, my poor Pnin, with hallucinatory sharpness, imagined Mira slipping out of there into the garden and coming toward him among tall tobacco flowers whose dull white mingled in the dark with that of her frock. This feeling coincided somehow with the sense of diffusion and dilation within his chest. Gently he laid his mallet aside and, to dissipate the anguish, started walking away from the house, through the silent pine grove. From a car which was parked near the garden tool house and which contained presumably at least two of his fellow guests' children, there issued a steady trickle of radio music.

"Jazz, jazz, they always must have their jazz, those youngsters," muttered Pnin to himself, and turned into the path that led to the forest and river. He remembered the fads of his and Mira's youth, the amateur theatricals, the gypsy ballads, the passion she had for photography. Where were they now, those artistic snapshots she used to take—pets, clouds, flowers, an April glade with shadows of birches on wet-sugar snow, soldiers posturing on the roof of a boxcar, a sunset skyline, a hand holding a book? He remembered the last day they had met, on the Neva embankment in Petrograd, and the tears, and the stars, and the warm rose-red silk lining of her karakul muff. The Civil War of 1918–22 separated them: history broke their engagement. Timofey wandered southward, to join briefly the ranks of Denikin's army, while Mira's family escaped from the Bolsheviks to Sweden and then settled down in Germany, where eventually she married a fur dealer of Russian extraction. Sometime in the early thirties, Pnin, by then married too, accompanied his wife to Berlin, where she wished to attend a congress of psychotherapists, and one night, at a Russian restaurant on the Kurfürstendamm, he saw Mira again. They exchanged a few words, she smiled at him in the remembered fashion, from under her dark brows, with that bashful slyness of hers; and the contour of her prominent cheekbones, and the elongated eyes, and the slenderness of arm and ankle were unchanged, were immortal, and then she joined her husband who was getting his overcoat at the cloakroom, and that was all—but the pang of tenderness remained, akin to the vibrating outline of verses you know you know but cannot recall.

What chatty Madam Shpolyanski mentioned had conjured up Mira's image with unusual force. This was disturbing. Only in the detachment of an incurable complaint, in the sanity of near death, could one cope with this for a moment. In order to exist rationally, Pnin had taught himself, during the last ten years, never to remember Mira Belochkin—not because, in itself, the evocation of a youthful love affair, banal and brief, threatened his peace of mind (alas, recollections of his

134

marriage to Liza were imperious enough to crowd out any former romance), but because, if one were quite sincere with oneself, no conscience, and hence no consciousness, could be expected to subsist in a world where such things as Mira's death were possible. One had to forget—because one could not live with the thought that this graceful, fragile, tender young woman with those eyes, that smile, those gardens and snows in the background, had been brought in a cattle car to an extermination camp and killed by an injection of phenol into the heart, into the gentle heart one had heard beating under one's lips in the dusk of the past. And since the exact form of her death had not been recorded, Mira kept dying a great number of deaths in one's mind, and undergoing a great number of resurrections, only to die again and again, led away by a trained nurse, inoculated with filth, tetanus bacilli, broken glass, gassed in a sham shower bath with prussic acid, burned alive in a pit on a gasoline-soaked pile of beechwood. According to the investigator Pnin had happened to talk to in Washington, the only certain thing was that being too weak to work (though still smiling, still able to help other Jewish women), she was selected to die and was cremated only a few days after her arrival in Buchenwald, in the beautifully wooded Grosser Ettersberg, as the region is resoundingly called. It is an hour's stroll from Weimar, where walked Goethe, Herder, Schiller, Wieland, the inimitable Kotzebue and others. "*Aber warum*—but why—" Dr. Hagen, the gentlest of souls alive, would wail, "why had one to put that horrid camp so near!" for indeed, it was near—only five miles from the cultural heart of Germany—"that nation of universities," as the President of Waindell College, re-

135

nowned for his use of the *mot juste,* had so elegantly phrased it when reviewing the European situation in a recent Commencement speech, along with the compliment he paid another torture house, "Russia—the country of Tolstoy, Stanislavski, Raskolnikov, and other great and good men."

Pnin slowly walked under the solemn pines. The sky was dying. He did not believe in an autocratic God. He did believe, dimly, in a democracy of ghosts. The souls of the dead, perhaps, formed committees, and these, in continuous session, attended to the destinies of the quick.

The mosquitoes were getting bothersome. Time for tea. Time for a game of chess with Chateau. That strange spasm was over, one could breathe again. On the distant crest of the knoll, at the exact spot where Gramineev's easel had stood a few hours before, two dark figures in profile were silhouetted against the ember-red sky. They stood there closely, facing each other. One could not make out from the road whether it was the Poroshin girl and her beau, or Nina Bolotov and young Poroshin, or merely an emblematic couple placed with easy art on the last page of Pnin's fading day.

Chapter Six

1

The 1954 Fall Term had begun. Again the marble neck of a homely Venus in the vestibule of Humanities Hall received the vermilion imprint, in applied lipstick, of a mimicked kiss. Again the *Waindell Recorder* discussed the Parking Problem. Again in the margins of library books earnest freshmen inscribed such helpful glosses as "Description of nature," or "Irony"; and in a pretty edition of Mallarmé's poems an especially able scholiast had already underlined in violet ink the difficult word *oiseaux* and scrawled above it "birds." Again autumn gales plastered dead leaves against one side of the latticed gallery leading from Humanities to Frieze Hall.

Again, on serene afternoons, huge, amber-brown Monarch butterflies flapped over asphalt and lawn as they lazily drifted south, their incompletely retracted black legs hanging rather low beneath their polka-dotted bodies.

And still the College creaked on. Hard-working graduates, with pregnant wives, still wrote dissertations on Dostoevski and Simone de Beauvoir. Literary departments still labored under the impression that Stendhal, Galsworthy, Dreiser, and Mann were great writers. Word plastics like "conflict" and "pattern" were still in vogue. As usual, sterile instructors successfully endeavored to "produce" by reviewing the books of more fertile colleagues, and, as usual, a crop of lucky faculty members were enjoying or about to enjoy various awards received earlier in the year. Thus, an amusing little grant was affording the versatile Starr couple— baby-faced Christopher Starr and his child-wife Louise —of the Fine Arts Department the unique opportunity of recording postwar folk songs in East Germany, into which these amazing young people had somehow obtained permission to penetrate. Tristram W. Thomas ("Tom" to his friends), Professor of Anthropology, had obtained ten thousand dollars from the Mandoville Foundation for a study of the eating habits of Cuban fishermen and palm climbers. Another charitable institution had come to the assistance of Dr. Bodo von Falternfels, to enable him to complete "a bibliography concerned with such published and manuscript material as has been devoted in recent years to a critical appraisal of the influence of Nietzsche's disciples on Modern Thought." And, last but not least, the bestowal of a particularly generous grant was allowing the renowned

Waindell psychiatrist, Dr. Rudolph Aura, to apply to ten thousand elementary school pupils the so-called Fingerbowl Test, in which the child is asked to dip his index in cups of colored fluids whereupon the proportion between length of digit and wetted part is measured and plotted in all kinds of fascinating graphs.

The Fall Term had begun, and Dr. Hagen was faced with a complicated situation. During the summer, he had been informally approached by an old friend about whether he might consider accepting next year a delightfully lucrative professorship at Seaboard, a far more important university than Waindell. This part of the problem was comparatively easy to solve. On the other hand, there remained the chilling fact that the department he had so lovingly built, with which Blorenge's French Department, although far richer in funds, could not vie in cultural impact, would be relinquished into the claws of treacherous Falternfels, whom he, Hagen, had obtained from Austria and who had turned against him—had actually managed to appropriate by underhand methods the direction of *Europa Nova*, an influential quarterly Hagen had founded in 1945. Hagen's proposed departure of which, as yet, he had divulged nothing to his colleagues—would have a still more heart-rending consequence: Assistant Professor Pnin must be left in the lurch. There had never been any regular Russian Department at Waindell and my poor friend's academic existence had always depended on his being employed by the eclectic German Department in a kind of Comparative Literature extension of one of its branches. Out of pure spite, Bodo was sure to lop off that limb, and Pnin, who had no life tenure at Waindell, would be forced to leave—unless some other literature-and-language Department agreed to adopt him. The only departments that seemed flexible enough to do so were those of English and French. But Jack Cockerell, Chairman of English, disapproved of everything Hagen did, considered Pnin a joke, and was, in fact, unofficially but hopefully haggling for the services of a prominent Anglo-Russian writer who, if necessary, could teach all the courses that Pnin must keep in order to survive. As a last resort, Hagen turned to Blorenge.

2

Two interesting characteristics distinguished Leonard Blorenge, Chairman of French Literature and Language; he disliked Literature and he had no French. This did not prevent him from traveling tremendous distances to attend Modern Language conventions, at which he would flaunt his ineptitude as if it were some majestic whim, and parry with great thrusts of healthy lodge humor any attempt to inveigle him into the subtleties of the parley-voo. A highly esteemed money-getter, he had recently induced a rich old man, whom three great universities had courted in vain, to promote with a fantastic endowment a riot of research conducted by graduates under the direction of Dr. Slavski, a Canadian, toward the erection on a hill near Waindell, of a "French Village," two streets and a square, to be copied from those of the ancient little burg of Vandel in the Dordogne. Despite the grandiose element always present in his administrative illuminations, Blorenge personally was a man of ascetic tastes. He had happened to go to school with Sam Poore, Waindell's President, and for many years, regularly, even after the latter had lost his sight, the two would go fishing together on a bleak, wind-raked lake, at the end of a gravel road lined with fireweed, seventy miles north of Waindell, in the kind of dreary brush country—scrub oak and nursery pine—that, in terms of nature, is the counterpart of a slum. His wife, a sweet woman of simple antecedents, referred to him at her club as "Professor Blorenge." He gave a course entitled "Great Frenchmen," which he had had his secretary copy out from a set of *The Hastings Historical and Philosophical Magazine* for 1882–94, discovered by him in an attic and not represented in the College Library.

3

Pnin had just rented a small house, and had invited the Hagens and the Clementses, and the Thayers, and Betty Bliss to a housewarming party. On the morning of that day, good Dr. Hagen made a desperate visit to Blorenge's office and revealed to him, and to him alone, the whole situation. When he told Blorenge that Falternfels was a strong anti-Pninist, Blorenge drily rejoined that so was he; in fact, after meeting Pnin socially, he "definitely felt" (it is truly a wonder how prone these practical people arc to feel rather than to think) that Pnin was not fit even to loiter in the vicinity of an American college. Staunch Hagen said that for several terms Pnin had been admirably dealing with the Romantic Movement and might surely handle Chateaubriand and Victor Hugo under the auspices of the French Department.

"Dr. Slavski takes care of that crowd," said Blorenge. "In fact, I sometimes think we overdo literature. Look, this week Miss Mopsuestia begins the Existentialists, your man Bodo does Romain Rolland, I lecture on General Boulanger and De Béranger. No, we have definitely enough of the stuff."

Hagen, playing his last card, suggested Pnin could teach a French language course: like many Russians, our friend had had a French governess as a child, and after the Revolution he lived in Paris for more than fifteen years.

"You mean," asked Blorenge sternly, "he can *speak* French?"

Hagen, who was well aware of Blorenge's special requirements, hesitated.

"Out with it, Herman! Yes or no?"

"I am sure he could adapt himself."

"He does speak it, eh?"

"Well, yes."

"In that case," said Blorenge, "we can't use him in First-Year French. It would be unfair to our Mr. Smith, who gives the elementary course this term and, naturally, is required to be only one lesson ahead of his students. Now it so happens that Mr. Hashimoto needs an assistant for his overflowing group in Intermediate French. Does your man *read* French as well as speak it?"

"I repeat, he can adapt himself," hedged Hagen.

"I know what adaptation means," said Blorenge, frowning. "In 1950, when Hash was away, I engaged that Swiss skiing instructor and he smuggled in mimeo copies of some old French anthology. It took us almost a year to bring the class back to its initial level. Now, if what's-his-name does not read French——"

"I'm afraid he does," said Hagen with a sigh.

"Then we can't use him at all. As you know, we believe only in speech records and other mechanical devices. No books are allowed."

"There still remains Advanced French," murmured Hagen.

"Carolina Slavski and I take care of that," answered Blorenge.

4

For Pnin, who was totally unaware of his protector's woes, the new Fall Term began particularly well: he had never had so few students to bother about, or so much time for his own research. This research had long entered the charmed stage when the quest overrides the goal, and a new organism is formed, the parasite so to speak of the ripening fruit. Pnin averted his mental gaze from the end of his work, which was so clearly in sight that one could make out the rocket of an asterisk, the flare of a "sic!" This line of land was to be shunned as the doom of everything that determined the rapture of endless approximation. Index cards were gradually loading a shoe box with their compact weight. The collation of two legends; a precious detail in manners or dress; a reference checked and found to be falsified by incompetence, carelessness, or fraud; the spine thrill of a felicitous guess; and all the innumerable triumphs of *bezkorïstnïy* (disinterested, devoted) scholarship—this had corrupted Pnin, this had made of him a happy, footnote-drugged maniac who disturbs the book mites in a dull volume, a foot thick, to find in it a reference to an even duller one. And on another, more human, plane there was the little brick house that he had rented on Todd Road, at the corner of Cliff Avenue.

143

It had lodged the family of the late Martin Sheppard, an uncle of Pnin's previous landlord in Creek Street and for many years the caretaker of the Todd property, which the town of Waindell had now acquired for the purpose of turning its rambling mansion into a modern nursing home. Ivy and spruce muffled its locked gate, whose top Pnin could see on the far side of Cliff Avenue from a north window of his new home. This avenue was the crossbar of a T, in the left crotch of which he dwelt. Opposite the front of his house, immediately across Todd Road (the upright of the T) old elms screened the sandy shoulder of its patched-up asphalt from a cornfield east of it, while along its west side a regiment of young fir trees, identical upstarts, walked, campus-ward, behind a fence, for almost the whole distance to the next residence—the Varsity Football Coach's magnified cigar box, which stood half a mile south from Pnin's house.

The sense of living in a discrete building all by himself was to Pnin something singularly delightful and amazingly satisfying to a weary old want of his innermost self, battered and stunned by thirty-five years of homelessness. One of the sweetest things about the place was the silence—angelic, rural, and perfectly secure, thus in blissful contrast to the persistent cacophonies that had surrounded him from six sides in the rented rooms of his former habitations. And the tiny house was so spacious! With grateful surprise, Pnin thought that had there been no Russian Revolution, no exodus, no expatriation in France, no naturalization in America, everything—at the best, at the best, Timofey! —would have been much the same: a professorship in Kharkov or Kazan, a suburban house such as this, old

144

books within, late blooms without. It was—to be more precise—a two-story house of cherry-red brick, with white shutters and a shingle roof. The green plat on which it stood had a frontage of about fifty arshins and was limited at the back by a vertical stretch of mossy cliff with tawny shrubs on its crest. A rudimentary driveway along the south side of the house led to a small whitewashed garage for the poor man's car Pnin owned. A curious basketlike net, somewhat like a glorified billiard pocket—lacking, however, a bottom—was suspended for some reason above the garage door, upon the white of which it cast a shadow as distinct as its own weave but larger and in a bluer tone. Pheasants visited the weedy ground between the garage and the cliff. Lilacs—those Russian garden graces, to whose springtime splendor, all honey and hum, my poor Pnin greatly looked forward—crowded in sapless ranks along one wall of the house. And a tall deciduous tree, which Pnin, a birch-lime-willow-aspen-poplar-oak man, was unable to identify, cast its large, heart-shaped, rust-colored leaves and Indian-summer shadows upon the wooden steps of the open porch.

A cranky-looking oil furnace in the basement did its best to send up its weak warm breath through registers in the floors. The kitchen looked healthy and gay, and Pnin had a great time with all kinds of cookware, kettles and pans, toasters and skillets, all of which came with the house. The living room was scantily and dingily furnished, but had a rather attractive bay harboring a huge old globe, where Russia was painted a pale blue, with a discolored or scrubbed patch all over Poland. In a very small dining room, where Pnin contemplated arranging a buffet supper for his guests, a pair of crystal candlesticks with pendants was responsible in the early mornings for iridescent reflections, which glowed charmingly on the sideboard and reminded my sentimental friend of the stained-glass casements that colored the sunlight orange and green and violet on the verandas of Russian country houses. A china closet, every time he passed by it, went into a rumbling act that also was somehow familiar from dim back rooms of the past. The second floor consisted of two bedrooms, both of which had been the abode of many small children, with incidental adults. The floors were chafed by tin toys. From the wall of the chamber Pnin decided to sleep in he had untacked a pennant-shaped red cardboard with the enigmatic word "Cardinals" daubed on it in white; but a tiny rocker for a three-year-old Pnin, painted pink, was allowed to remain in its corner. A disabled sewing machine occupied a passageway leading to the bathroom, where the usual short tub, made for dwarfs by a nation of giants, took as long to fill as the tanks and basins of the arithmetic in Russian school books.

He was now ready to give that party. The living room had a sofa that could seat three, there were two wing-back chairs, an overstuffed easy chair, a chair with a rush seat, one hassock, and two footstools. All of a sudden he experienced an odd feeling of dissatisfaction as he checked the little list of his guests. It had body but it lacked bouquet. Of course, he was tremendously fond of the Clementses (real people—not like most of the campus dummies), with whom he had had such exhilarating talks in the days when he was their roomer; of course, he felt very grateful to Herman Hagen for many a good turn, such as that raise Hagen had recently arranged; of course, Mrs. Hagen was, in Waindell parlance, "a lovely person"; of course, Mrs. Thayer was always so helpful at the library, and her husband had such a soothing capacity for showing how silent a man could be if he strictly avoided comments on the weather. But there was nothing extraordinary, nothing original, about this combination of people, and old Pnin recalled those birthday parties in his boyhood— the half a dozen children invited who were somehow always the same, and the pinching shoes, and the aching temples, and the kind of heavy, unhappy, constraining dullness that would settle on him after all the games had been played and a rowdy cousin had started putting nice new toys to vulgar and stupid uses; and he also recalled the lone buzz in his ears when, in the course of a protracted hide-and-seek routine, after an hour of uncomfortable concealment, he emerged from a dark and stuffy wardrobe in the maid's chamber, only to find that all his playmates had already gone home.

While visiting a famous grocery between Waindelville and Isola, he ran into Betty Bliss, asked her, and she said she still remembered Turgenev's prose poem about roses, with its refrain "*Kak horoshi, kak svezhi* (How fair, how fresh)," and would certainly be delighted to come. He asked the celebrated mathematician, Professor Idelson, and his wife, the sculptress, and they said they would come with joy but later telephoned to say they were tremendously sorry—they had overlooked a previous engagement. He asked young Miller, by now an Associate Professor, and Charlotte, his pretty, freckled wife, but it turned out she was on the point of having a baby. He asked old Carrol, the Frieze Hall head janitor, with his son Frank, who had

147

been my friend's only talented student and had written a brilliant doctor's thesis for him on the relationship between Russian, English, and German iambics; but Frank was in the army, and old Carrol confessed that "the missus and I do not mix much with the profs." He rang up the residence of President Poore, whom he had once talked to (about improving the curriculum) at a lawn function, until it started to rain, and asked him to come, but President Poore's niece answered that her uncle nowadays "never visits with anybody except a few personal friends." He was about to give up the notion of enlivening his list, when a perfectly new and really admirable idea occurred to him.

5

Pnin and I had long since accepted the disturbing but seldom discussed fact that on any given college staff one could find not only a person who was uncommonly like one's dentist or the local postmaster, but also a person who had a twin within the same professional group. I know, indeed, of a case of triplets at a comparatively small college where, according to its sharp-eyed president, Frank Reade, the radix of the troika was, absurdly enough, myself; and I recall the late Olga Krotki once telling me that among the fifty or so faculty members of a wartime Intensive Language School, at which the poor, one-lunged lady had to teach Lethean and Fenugreek, there were as many as six Pnins, besides the genuine and, to me, unique article. It should not be deemed surprising, therefore, that even Pnin, not a very observant man in everyday life, could not help becoming aware (sometime during his ninth year at Waindell) that a lanky, bespectacled old fellow with scholarly strands of steel-gray hair falling over the right side of his small but corrugated brow, and with a deep furrow descending from each side of his sharp nose to each corner of his long upper-lip—a person whom Pnin knew as Professor Thomas Wynn, Head of the Ornithology Department, having once talked to him at some party about gay golden orioles, melancholy cuckoos, and other Russian countryside birds—was not always Professor Wynn. At times he graded, as it were, into somebody else, whom Pnin did not know by name but whom he classified, with a bright foreigner's fondness for puns as "Twynn" (or, in Pninian, "Tvin"). My friend and compatriot soon realized that he could never be sure whether the owlish, rapidly stalking gentleman, whose path he would cross every other day at different points of progress, between office and classroom, between classroom and stairs, between drinking fountain and lavatory, was really his chance acquaintance, the ornithologist, whom he felt bound to greet in passing, or the Wynn-like stranger, who acknowledged that somber salute with exactly the same degree of automatic politeness as any chance acquaintance would. The moment of meeting would be very brief, since both Pnin and Wynn (or Twynn) walked fast; and sometimes Pnin, in order to avoid the exchange of urbane barks, would feign reading a letter on the run, or would manage to dodge his rapidly advancing colleague and tormentor by swerving into a stairway and then continuing along a lower-floor corridor; but no sooner had he begun to rejoice in the smartness of the device than upon using it one day he almost collided with Tvin (or Vin) pounding along the subjacent passage. When the new

Fall Term (Pnin's tenth) began, the nuisance was aggravated by the fact that Pnin's class hours had been changed, thus abolishing certain trends on which he had been learning to rely in his efforts to elude Wynn and Wynn's simulator. It seemed he would have to endure it always. For recalling certain other duplications in the past—disconcerting likenesses he alone had seen—bothered Pnin told himself it would be useless to ask anybody's assistance in unraveling the T. Wynns.

On the day of his party, as he was finishing a late lunch in Frieze Hall, Wynn, or his double, neither of whom had ever appeared there before, suddenly sat down beside him and said:

"I have long wanted to ask you something—you teach Russian, don't you? Last summer I was reading a magazine article on birds——"

("Vin! This is Vin!" said Pnin to himself, and forthwith perceived a decisive course of action).

"—well, the author of that article—I don't remember his name, I think it was a Russian one—mentioned that in the Skoff region, I hope I pronounce it right, a local cake is baked in the form of a bird. Basically, of course, the symbol is phallic, but I was wondering if you knew of such a custom?"

It was then that the brilliant idea flashed in' Pnin's mind.

"Sir, I am at your service," he said with a note of exultation quivering in his throat—for he now saw his way to pin down definitely the personality of at least the initial Wynn who liked birds. "Yes, sir. I know all about those *zhavoronki*, those *alouettes*, those—we must consult a dictionary for the English name. So I take the opportunity to extend a cordial invitation to you to visit me this evening. Half past eight, postmeridian. A little house-heating soiree, nothing more. Bring also your spouse—or perhaps you are a Bachelor of Hearts?"

(Oh, punster Pnin!)

His interlocutor said he was not married. He would love to come. What was the address?

"It is nine hundred ninety nine, Todd Rodd, very simple! At the very very end of the rodd, where it unites with Cleef Ahvnue. A leetle breek house and a beeg blahk cleef."

6

That afternoon Pnin could hardly wait to start culinary operations. He began them soon after five and only interrupted them to don, for the reception of his guests, a sybaritic smoking jacket of blue silk, with tasseled belt and satin lapels, won at an émigré charity bazaar in Paris twenty years ago—how the time flies! This jacket he wore with a pair of old tuxedo trousers, likewise of European origin. Peering at himself in the cracked mirror of the medicine chest, he put on his heavy tortoise-shell reading glasses, from under the saddle of which his Russian potato nose smoothly bulged. He bared his synthetic teeth. He inspected his cheeks and chin to see if his morning shave still held. It did. With finger and thumb he grasped a long nostril hair, plucked it out after a second hard tug, and sneezed lustily, an "Ah!" of well-being rounding out the explosion.

At half past seven Betty arrived to help with final arrangements. Betty now taught English and History at Isola High School. She had not changed since the days when she was a buxom graduate student. Her pink-rimmed myopic gray eyes peered at you with the same ingenuous sympathy. She wore the same Gretchen-like coil of thick hair around her head. There was the same scar on her soft throat. But an engagement ring with a diminutive diamond had appeared on her plump hand, and this she displayed with coy pride to Pnin, who vaguely experienced a twinge of sadness. He reflected that there was a time he might have courted her—would have done so, in fact, had she not had a servant maid's mind, which had remained unaltered too. She could still relate a long story on a "she said-I said-she said" basis. Nothing on earth could make her disbelieve in the wisdom and wit of her favorite woman's magazine. She still had the curious trick—shared by two or three other small-town young women within Pnin's limited ken—of giving you a delayed little tap on the sleeve in acknowledgment of, rather than in retaliation for, any remark reminding her of some minor lapse: you would say, "Betty, you forgot to return that book," or "I thought, Betty, you said you would never marry," and before she actually answered, there it would come, that demure gesture, retracted at the very moment her stubby fingers came into contact with your wrist.

"He is a biochemist and is now in Pittsburgh," said Betty as she helped Pnin to arrange buttered slices of French bread around a pot of glossy-gray fresh caviar and to rinse three large bunches of grapes. There was also a large plate of cold cuts, real German pumpernickel, and a dish of very special vinaigrette, where shrimps hobnobbed with pickles and peas, and some miniature sausages in tomato sauce, and hot *pirozhki* (mushroom tarts, meat tarts, cabbage tarts), and four kinds of nuts, and various interesting Oriental sweets. Drinks were to be represented by whisky (Betty's contribution), *ryabinovka* (a rowanberry liqueur), brandy-and-grenadine cocktails, and of course Pnin's Punch, a heady mixture of chilled Chateau Yquem, grapefruit juice, and maraschino, which the solemn host had already started to stir in a large bowl of brilliant aquamarine glass with a decorative design of swirled ribbing and lily pads.

"My, what a lovely thing!" cried Betty.

Pnin eyed the bowl with pleased surprise as if seeing it for the first time. It was, he said, a present from Victor. Yes, how was he, how did he like St. Bart's? He liked it so-so. He had passed the beginning of the summer in California with his mother, then had worked two months at a Yosemite hotel. A *what*? A hotel in the Californian mountains. Well, he had returned to his school and had suddenly sent this.

By some tender coincidence the bowl had come on the very day Pnin had counted the chairs and started to plan this party. It had come enclosed in a box within another box inside a third one, and wrapped up in an extravagant mass of excelsior and paper that had spread all over the kitchen like a carnival storm. The bowl that emerged was one of those gifts whose first impact produces in the recipient's mind a colored image, a blazoned blur, reflecting with such emblematic force the sweet nature of the donor that the tangible attributes of the thing are dissolved, as it were, in this pure inner blaze, but suddenly and forever leap into brilliant being when praised by an outsider to whom the true glory of the object is unknown.

A musical tinkle reverberated through the small house, and the Clementses entered with a bottle of French champagne and a cluster of dahlias.

Dark-blue-eyed, long-lashed, bob-haired Joan wore an old black silk dress that was smarter than anything other faculty wives could devise, and it was always a pleasure to watch good old bald Tim Pnin bend slightly to touch with his lips the light hand that Joan, alone of all the Waindell ladies, knew how to raise to exactly the right level for a Russian gentleman to kiss. Laurence, fatter than ever, dressed in nice gray flannels, sank into the easy chair and immediately grabbed the first book at hand, which happened to be an English-Russian and Russian-English pocket dictionary. Holding his glasses in one hand, he looked away, trying to recall something he had always wished to check but now could not remember, and his attitude accentuated his striking resemblance, somewhat *en jeune*, to Jan van Eyck's ample-jowled, fluff-haloed Canon van der Paele, seized by a fit of abstraction in the presence of the puzzled Virgin to whom a super, rigged up as St. George, is directing the good Canon's attention. Everything was there—the knotty temple, the sad, musing gaze, the folds and furrows of facial flesh, the thin lips, and even the wart on the left cheek.

Hardly had the Clementses settled down than Betty let in the man interested in bird-shaped cakes. Pnin was about to say "Professor Vin" but Joan—rather unfortunately, perhaps—interrupted the introduction with "Oh, we know Thomas! Who does not know Tom?" Tim

Pnin returned to the kitchen, and Betty handed around some Bulgarian cigarettes.

"I thought, Thomas," remarked Clements, crossing his fat legs, "you were out in Havana interviewing palm-climbing fishermen?"

"Well, I'll be on my way after midyears," said Professor Thomas. "Of course, most of the actual field work has been done already by others."

"Still, it was nice to get that grant, wasn't it?"

"In our branch," replied Thomas with perfect composure, "we have to undertake many difficult journeys. In fact, I may push on to the Windward Islands. If," he added with a hollow laugh, "Senator McCarthy does not crack down on foreign travel."

"He received a grant of ten thousand dollars," said Joan to Betty, whose face dropped a curtsy as she made that special grimace consisting of a slow half-bow and tensing of chin and lower lip that automatically conveys, on the part of Bettys, a respectful, congratulatory, and slightly awed recognition of such grand things as dining with one's boss, being in *Who's Who,* or meeting a duchess.

The Thayers, who came in a new station wagon, presented their host with an elegant box of mints. Dr. Hagen, who came on foot, triumphantly held aloft a bottle of vodka.

"Good evening, good evening, good evening," said hearty Hagen.

"Dr. Hagen," said Thomas as he shook hands with him. "I hope the Senator did not see you walking about with that stuff."

The good Doctor had perceptibly aged since last year but was as sturdy and square-shaped as ever with his well-padded shoulders, square chin, square nostrils, leonine glabella, and rectangular brush of grizzled hair that had something topiary about it. He wore a black suit over a white nylon shirt, and a black tie with a red thunderbolt streaking down it. Mrs. Hagen had been prevented from coming, at the very last moment, by a dreadful migraine, alas.

Pnin served the cocktails "or better to say flamingo tails—specially for ornithologists," as he slyly quipped.

"Thank you!" chanted Mrs. Thayer, as she received her glass, raising her linear eyebrows, on that bright note of genteel inquiry which is meant to combine the notions of surprise, unworthiness, and pleasure. An attractive, prim, pink-faced lady of forty or so, with pearly dentures and wavy goldenized hair, she was the provincial cousin of the smart, relaxed Joan Clements, who had been all over the world, even in Turkey and Egypt, and was married to the most original and least liked scholar on the Waindell campus. A good word should be also put in at this point for Margaret Thayer's husband, Roy, a mournful and mute member of the Department of English, which, except for its ebullient chairman, Cockerell, was an aerie of hypochondriacs. Outwardly, Roy was an obvious figure. If you drew a pair of old brown loafers, two beige elbow patches, a black pipe, and two baggy eyes under heavy eyebrows, the rest was easy to fill out. Somewhere in the middle distance hung an obscure liver ailment, and somewhere in the background there was Eighteenth-Century Poetry, Roy's particular field, an overgrazed pasture, with the trickle of a brook and a clump of initialed trees; a barbed-wire arrangement on either side of this field separated it from Professor Stowe's domain, the preceding century, where the lambs were whiter, the turf softer, the rill purlier, and from Dr. Shapiro's early nineteenth century, with its glen mists, sea fogs, and imported grapes. Roy Thayer avoided talking of his subject, avoided, in fact, talking of any subject, had squandered a decade of gray life on an erudite work dealing with a forgotten group of unnecessary poetasters, and kept a detailed diary, in cryptogrammed verse, which he hoped posterity would someday decipher and, in sober backcast, proclaim the greatest literary achievement of our time—and for all I know, Roy Thayer, you might be right.

When everybody was comfortably lapping and lauding the cocktails, Professor Pnin sat down on the wheezy hassock near his newest friend and said:

"I have to report, sir, on the skylark, *zhavoronok* in Russian, about which you made me the honor to interrogate me. Take this with you to your home. I have here tapped on the typewriting machine a condensed account with bibliography. I think we will now transport ourselves to the other room where a supper *à la fourchette* is, I think, awaiting us."

8

Presently, guests with full plates drifted back into the parlor. The punch was brought in.

"Gracious, Timofey, where on earth did you get that perfectly divine bowl!" exclaimed Joan.

"Victor presented it to me."

"But where did he *get* it?"

"Antiquaire store in Cranton, I think."

"Gosh, it must have cost a fortune."

"One dollar? Ten dollars? Less maybe?"

"Ten dollars—nonsense! Two hundred, I should say. *Look* at it! Look at this writhing pattern. You know, you should show it to the Cockerells. They know everything about old glass. In fact, they have a Lake Dunmore pitcher that looks like a poor relation of this."

Margaret Thayer admired it in her turn, and said that when she was a child, she imagined Cinderella's glass shoes to be exactly of that greenish blue tint; whereupon Professor Pnin remarked that, *primo,* he would like everybody to say if contents were as good as container, and, *secundo,* that Cendrillon's shoes were not made of glass but of Russian squirrel fur—*vair,* in French. It was, he said, an obvious case of the survival of the fittest among words, *verre* being more evocative than *vair* which, he submitted, came not from *varius,* variegated, but from *veveritsa,* Slavic for a certain beautiful, pale, winter-squirrel fur, having a bluish, or better say *sizily,* columbine, shade—from *columba,* Latin for "pigeon," as somebody here well knows—so you see, Mrs. Fire, you were, in general, correct."

"The contents are fine," said Laurence Clements.

"This beverage is certainly delicious," said Margaret Thayer.

("I always thought 'columbine' was some sort of flower," said Thomas to Betty, who lightly acquiesced.)

The respective ages of several children were then passed in review. Victor would be fifteen soon. Eileen, the granddaughter of Mrs. Thayer's eldest sister, was five. Isabel was twenty-three and greatly enjoying a secretarial job in New York. Dr. Hagen's daughter was twenty-four, and about to return from Europe, where she had spent a wonderful summer touring Bavaria and

Switzerland with a very gracious old lady, Dorianna Karen, famous movie star of the twenties.

The telephone rang. Somebody wanted to talk to Mrs. Sheppard. With a precision quite unusual for him in such matters, unpredictable Pnin not only rattled off the woman's new address and telephone number, but also supplied those of her eldest son.

9

By ten o'clock, Pnin's Punch and Betty's scotch were causing some of the guests to talk louder than they thought they did. A carmine flush had spread over one side of Mrs. Thayer's neck, under the little blue star of her left earring, and, sitting very straight, she regaled her host with an account of the feud between two of her co-workers at the library. It was a simple office story, but her changes of tone from Miss Shrill to Mr. Basso, and the consciousness of the soiree going on so nicely, made Pnin bend his head and guffaw ecstatically behind his hand. Roy Thayer was weakly twinkling to himself as he looked into his punch, down his gray porous nose, and politely listened to Joan Clements who, when she was a little high as she was now, had a fetching way of rapidly blinking, or even completely closing her black-lashed blue eyes, and of interrupting her sentences, to punctuate a clause or gather new momentum, by deep hawing pants: "But don't you think—haw—that what he is trying to do—haw—practically in all his novels—haw—is—haw—to express the fantastic recurrence of certain situations?" Betty remained her controlled little self, and expertly looked after the refreshments. In the bay end of the room, Clements kept morosely revolving the slow globe as Hagen, carefully avoiding the traditional intonations he would have used in more congenial surroundings, told him and grinning Thomas the latest story about Mrs. Idelson, communicated by Mrs. Blorenge to Mrs. Hagen. Pnin came up with a plate of nougat.

"This is not quite for your chaste ears, Timofey," said Hagen to Pnin, who always confessed he never could see the point of any "scabrous anecdote." "However—"

Clements moved away to rejoin the ladies. Hagen began to retell the story, and Thomas began to re-grin. Pnin waved a hand at the raconteur in a Russian disgusted "oh-go-on-with-you" gesture and said:

"I have heard quite the same anecdote thirty-five years ago in Odessa, and even then I could not understand what is comical in it."

10

At a still later stage of the party, certain rearrangements had again taken place. In a corner of the davenport, bored Clements was flipping through an album of *Flemish Masterpieces* that Victor had been given by his mother and had left with Pnin. Joan sat on a footstool, at her husband's knee, a plate of grapes in the lap of her wide skirt, wondering when would it be time to go without hurting Timofey's feelings. The others were listening to Hagen discussing modern education:

"You may laugh," he said, casting a sharp glance at Clements—who shook his head, denying the charge, and then passed the album to Joan, pointing out something in it that had suddenly provoked his glee.

"You may laugh, but I affirm that the only way to escape from the morass—just a drop, Timofey: that will do—is to lock up the student in a soundproof cell and eliminate the lecture room."

"Yes, that's it," said Joan to her husband under her breath, handing the album back to him.

"I am glad you agree, Joan," continued Hagen. "However, I have been called an *enfant terrible* for expounding this theory, and perhaps you will not go on agreeing so easily when you hear me out. Phonograph records on every possible subject will be at the isolated student's disposal . . ."

"But the personality of the lecturer," said Margaret Thayer. "Surely that counts for something."

"It does not!" shouted Hagen. "That is the tragedy! Who, for example, wants *him*"—he pointed to radiant Pnin—"who wants his personality? Nobody! They will reject Timofey's wonderful personality without a quaver. The world wants a machine, not a Timofey."

"One could have Timofey televised," said Clements.

"Oh, I would love that," said Joan, beaming at her host, and Betty nodded vigorously. Pnin bowed deeply to them with an "I-am-disarmed" spreading of both hands.

"And what do *you* think of my controversial plan?" asked Hagen of Thomas.

"I can tell you what Tom thinks," said Clements, still contemplating the same picture in the book that lay open on his knees. "Tom thinks that the best method of teaching anything is to rely on discussion in class, which means letting twenty young blockheads and two cocky neurotics discuss for fifty minutes something that neither their teacher nor they know. Now, for the last three months," he went on, without any logical transition, "I have been looking for this picture, and here it is. The publisher of my new book on the Philosophy of Gesture wants a portrait of me, and Joan and I knew we had seen somewhere a stunning likeness by an Old Master but could not even recall his period. Well, here it is, here it is. The only retouching needed would be the addition of a sport shirt and the deletion of this warrior's hand."

"I must really protest," began Thomas.

Clements passed the open book to Margaret Thayer, and she burst out laughing.

"I must protest, Laurence," said Tom. "A relaxed discussion in an atmosphere of broad generalizations is a more realistic approach to education than the old-fashioned formal lecture."

"Sure, sure," said Clements.

Joan scrambled up to her feet and covered her glass with her narrow palm when Pnin offered to replenish it. Mrs. Thayer looked at her wrist watch, and then at her husband. A soft yawn distended Laurence's mouth. Betty asked Thomas if he knew a man called Fogelman, an expert in bats, who lived in Santa Clara, Cuba. Hagen asked for a glass of water or beer. Whom does he remind me of? thought Pnin suddenly. Eric Wind? Why? They are quite different physically.

11

The setting of the final scene was the hallway. Hagen could not find the cane he had come with (it had fallen behind a trunk in the closet).

"And *I* think I left my purse where I was sitting," said

Mrs. Thayer, pushing her pensive husband ever so slightly toward the living room.

Pnin and Clements, in last-minute discourse, stood on either side of the living-room doorway, like two well-fed caryatides, and drew in their abdomens to let the silent Thayer pass. In the middle of the room Professor Thomas and Miss Bliss—he with his hands behind his back and rising up every now and then on his toes, she holding a tray—were standing and talking of Cuba, where a cousin of Betty's fiancé had lived for quite a while, Betty understood. Thayer blundered from chair to chair, and found himself with a white bag, not knowing really where he picked it up, his mind being occupied by the adumbrations of lines he was to write down later in the night:

We sat and drank, each with a separate past locked up in him, and fate's alarm clocks set at unrelated futures—when, at last, a wrist was cocked, and eyes of consorts met . . .

Meanwhile Pnin asked Joan Clements and Margaret Thayer if they would care to see how he had embellished the upstairs rooms. The idea enchanted them. He led the way. His so called *kabinet* now looked very cozy, its scratched floor snugly covered with the more or less Pakistan rug which he had once acquired for his office and had recently removed in drastic silence from under the feet of the surprised Falternfels. A tartan lap robe, under which Pnin had crossed the ocean from Europe in 1940, and some endemic cushions disguised the unremovable bed. The pink shelves, which he had found supporting several generations of children's books—from *Tom the Bootblack, or the Road to Success* by Horatio Alger, Jr., 1889, through *Rolf in the Woods* by Ernest Thompson Seton, 1911, to a 1928 edition of *Compton's Pictured Encyclopedia* in ten volumes with foggy little photographs—were now loaded with three hundred sixty-five items from the Waindell College Library.

"And to think I have stamped all these," sighed Mrs. Thayer, rolling her eyes in mock dismay.

"Some stamped Mrs. Miller," said Pnin, a stickler for historical truth.

What struck the visitors most in the bedroom was a large folding screen that cut off the fourposter bed from insidious drafts, and the view from the row of small windows: a dark rock wall rising abruptly some fifty feet away, with a stretch of pale starry sky above the black growth of its crest. On the back lawn, across the reflection of a window, Laurence strolled into the shadows.

"At last you are really comfortable," said Joan.

"And you know what I will say to you," replied Pnin in a confidential undertone vibrating with triumph. "Tomorrow morning, under the curtain of mysteree, I will see a gentleman who is wanting to help me to buy this house!"

They came down again. Roy handed his wife Betty's bag. Herman found his cane. Margaret's bag was sought. Laurence reappeared.

"Good-by, good-by, Professor Vin!" sang out Pnin, his cheeks ruddy and round in the lamplight of the porch.

(Still in the hallway, Betty and Margaret Thayer admired proud Dr. Hagen's walking stick, recently sent him from Germany, a gnarled cudgel, with a donkey's head for knob. The head could move one ear. The cane had belonged to Dr. Hagen's Bavarian grand-father, a country clergyman. The mechanism of the other ear had broken down in 1914, according to a note the pastor had left. Hagen carried it, he said, in defense against a certain Alsatian in Greenlawn Lane. American dogs were not used to pedestrians. He always preferred walking to driving. The ear could not be repaired. At least, in Waindell.)

"Now I wonder why he called me that," said T. W. Thomas, Professor of Anthropology, to Laurence and Joan Clements as they walked through blue darkness toward four cars parked under the elms on the other side of the road.

"Our friend," answered Clements, "employs a nomen-clature all his own. His verbal vagaries add a new thrill to life. His mispronunciations are mythopeic. His slips of the tongue are oracular. He calls my wife John."

"Still I find it a little disturbing," said Thomas.

"He probably mistook you for somebody else," said Clements. "And for all I know you *may* be somebody else."

Before they had crossed the street they were over-taken by Dr. Hagen. Professor Thomas, still looking puzzled, took his leave.

"Well," said Hagen.

It was a fair fall night, velvet below, steel above.

Joan asked:

"You're sure you don't want us to give you a lift?"

"It's a ten-minute walk. And a walk is a must on such a wonderful night."

The three of them stood for a moment gazing at the stars.

"And all these are worlds," said Hagen.

"Or else," said Clements with a yawn, "a frightful mess. I suspect it is really a fluorescent corpse, and we are inside it."

From the lighted porch came Pnin's rich laughter as he finished recounting to the Thayers and Betty Bliss how he, too, had once retrieved the wrong reticule.

"Come, my fluorescent corpse, let's be moving," said Joan. "It was so nice to see you, Herman. Give my love to Irmgard. What a delightful party. I have never seen Timofey so happy."

"Yes, thank you," answered Hagen absent-mindedly.

"You should have seen his face," said Joan, "when he told us he was going to talk to a real-estate man tomorrow about buying that dream house."

"He did? You're sure he said that?" Hagen asked sharply.

"Quite sure," said Joan. "And if anybody needs a house, it is certainly Timofey."

"Well, good night," said Hagen. "Glad you could come. Good night."

He waited for them to reach their car, hesitated, and then marched back to the lighted porch, where, standing as on a stage, Pnin was shaking hands a second or third time with the Thayers and Betty.

("I would never," said Joan, as she backed the car and worked on the wheel, "but *never* have allowed my child to go abroad with that old Lesbian." "Careful," said Laurence, "he may be drunk but he is not out of earshot.")

"I shall not forgive you," said Betty to her merry host, "for not letting me do the dishes."

"I'll help him," said Hagen, ascending the porch steps

166

and thumping upon them with his cane. "You, children, run along now."

There was a final round of handshakes, and the Thayers and Betty left.

12

"First," said Hagen, as he and Pnin re-entered the living room, "I guess I'll have a last cup of wine with you."

"Perfect. Perfect!" cried Pnin. "Let us finish my *cruchon*."

They made themselves comfortable, and Dr. Hagen said:

"You are a wonderful host, Timofey. This is a very delightful moment. My grandfather used to say that a glass of good wine should be always sipped and savored as if it were the last one before the execution. I wonder what you put into this punch. I also wonder if, as our charming Joan affirms, you are really contemplating buying this house?"

"Not contemplating—peeping a little at possibilities," replied Pnin with a gurgling laugh.

"I question the wisdom of it," continued Hagen, nursing his goblet.

"Naturally, I am expecting that I will get tenure at last," said Pnin rather slyly. "I am now Assistant Professor nine years. Years run. Soon I will be Assistant Emeritus. Hagen, why are you silent?"

"You place me in a very embarrassing position, Timofey. I hoped you would not raise this particular question."

"I do not raise the question. I say that I only expect—oh, not next year, but example given, at hundredth anniversary of Liberation of Serfs—Waindell will make me Associate."

"Well, you see, my dear friend, I must tell you a sad secret. It is not official yet, and you must promise not to mention it to anyone."

"I swear," said Pnin, raising his hand.

"You cannot but know," continued Hagen, "with what loving care I built our great department. I, too, am no longer young. You say, Timofey, you have been here for nine years. But I have been giving my all for *twenty-nine* years to this university! My modest all. As my friend, Dr. Kraft, wrote me the other day: you, Herman Hagen, have done alone more for Germany in America than all our missions have done in Germany for America. And what happens now? I have nursed this Falternfels, this dragon, in my bosom, and he has now worked himself into a key position. I spare you the details of the intrigue!"

"Yes," said Pnin with a sigh, "intrigue is horrible, horrible. But, on the other side, honest work will always prove its advantage. You and I will give next year some splendid new courses which I have planned long ago. On Tyranny. On the Boot. On Nicholas the First. On all the precursors of modern atrocity. Hagen, when we speak of injustice, we forget Armenian massacres, tortures which Tibet invented, colonists in Africa. . . . The history of man is the history of pain!"

Hagen bent over to his friend and patted him on his knobby knee.

"You are a wonderful romantic, Timofey, and under happier circumstances . . . However, I can tell you that in the Spring Term we *are* going to do something unusual. We are going to stage a Dramatic Program—

168

scenes from Kotzebue to Hauptmann. I see it as a sort of apotheosis. . . . But let us not anticipate. I, too, am a romantic, Timofey, and therefore cannot work with people like Bodo, as our trustees wish me to do. Kraft is retiring at Seaboard, and it has been offered to me that I replace him, beginning next fall."

"I congratulate you," said Pnin warmly.

"Thanks, my friend. It is certainly a very fine and prominent position. I shall apply to a wider field of scholarship and administration the invaluable experience I have gained here. Of course, since I know Bodo will not continue you in the German Department, my first move was to suggest you come with me, but they tell me they have enough Slavists at Seaboard without you. So I spoke to Blorenge, but the French Department here is also full up. This is unfortunate, because Waindell feels that it would be too much of a financial burden to pay you for two or three Russian courses that have ceased to attract students. Political trends in America, as we all know, discourage interest in things Russian. On the other hand, you'll be glad to know that the English Department is inviting one of your most brilliant compatriots, a really fascinating lecturer—I have heard him once; I think he's an old friend of yours."

Pnin cleared his throat and asked:

"It signifies that they are firing me?"

"Now, don't take it too hard, Timofey. I'm sure your old friend—"

"Who is old friend?" queried Pnin, slitting his eyes.

Hagen named the fascinating lecturer.

Leaning forward, his elbows propped on his knees, clasping and unclasping his hands, Pnin said:

"Yes, I know him thirty years or more. We are friends, but there is one thing perfectly certain. I will never work under him."

"Well, I guess you should sleep on it. Perhaps some solution may be found. Anyway, we'll have ample opportunity to discuss these matters. We shall just go on teaching, you and I, as if nothing had happened, *nicht wahr*? We must be brave, Timofey!"

"So they have fired me," said Pnin, clasping his hands and nodding his head.

"Yes, we are in the same boat, in the same boat," said jovial Hagen, and he stood up. It was getting very late.

"I go now," said Hagen, who, though a lesser addict of the present tense than Pnin, also held it in favor. "It has been a wonderful party, and I would never have allowed myself to spoil the merriment if our mutual friend had not informed me of your optimistic intentions. Good night. Oh, by the way . . . Naturally, you will get your salary for the Fall Term in full, and then we shall see how much we can obtain for you in the Spring Term, especially if you will agree to take off some stupid office work from my poor old shoulders, and also if you will participate vitally in the Dramatic Program in New Hall. I think you should actually play in it, under my daughter's direction; it would distract you from sad thoughts. Now go to bed at once, and put yourself to sleep with a good mystery story."

On the porch he pumped Pnin's unresponsive hand with enough vigor for two. Then he flourished his cane and merrily marched down the wooden steps.

The screen door banged behind him.

"*Der arme Kerl*," muttered kindhearted Hagen to

himself as he walked homeward. "At least, I have sweetened the pill."

13

From the sideboard and dining-room table Pnin removed to the kitchen sink the used china and silverware. He put away what food remained into the bright Arctic light of the refrigerator. The ham and tongue had all gone, and so had the little sausages; but the vinaigrette had not been a success, and enough caviar and meat tarts were left over for a meal or two tomorrow. "Boom-boom-boom," said the china closet as he passed by. He surveyed the living room and started to tidy it up. A last drop of Pnin's Punch glistened in its beautiful bowl. Joan had crooked a lipstick-stained cigarette butt in her saucer; Betty had left no trace and had taken all the glasses back to the kitchen. Mrs. Thayer had forgotten a booklet of pretty multicolored matches on her plate, next to a bit of nougat. Mr. Thayer had twisted into all kinds of weird shapes half a dozen paper napkins; Hagen had quenched a messy cigar in an uneaten bunchlet of grapes.

In the kitchen, Pnin prepared to wash up the dishes. He removed his silk coat, his tie, and his dentures. To protect his shirt front and tuxedo trousers, he donned a soubrette's dappled apron. He scraped various tidbits off the plates into a brown paper bag, to be given eventually to a mangy little white dog, with pink patches on its back, that visited him sometimes in the afternoon—there was no reason a human's misfortune should interfere with a canine's pleasure.

He prepared a bubble bath in the sink for the crockery, glass, and silverware, and with infinite care

171

lowered the aquamarine bowl into the tepid foam. Its resonant flint glass emitted a sound full of muffled mellowness as it settled down to soak. He rinsed the amber goblets and the silverware under the tap, and submerged them in the same foam. Then he fished out the knives, forks, and spoons, rinsed them, and began to wipe them. He worked very slowly, with a certain vagueness of manner that might have been taken for a mist of abstraction in a less methodical man. He gathered the wiped spoons into a posy, placed them in a pitcher which he had washed but not dried, and then took them out one by one and wiped them all over again. He groped under the bubbles, around the goblets, and under the melodious bowl, for any piece of forgotten silver—and retrieved a nutcracker. Fastidious Pnin rinsed it, and was wiping it, when the leggy thing somehow slipped out of the towel and fell like a man from a roof. He almost caught it—his fingertips actually came into contact with it in mid-air, but this only helped to propel it into the treasure-concealing foam of the sink, where an excruciating crack of broken glass followed upon the plunge.

Pnin hurled the towel into a corner and, turning away, stood for a moment staring at the blackness beyond the threshold of the open back door. A quiet, lacy-winged little green insect circled in the glare of a strong naked lamp above Pnin's glossy bald head. He looked very old, with his toothless mouth half open and a film of tears dimming his blank, unblinking eyes. Then, with a moan of anguished anticipation, he went back to the sink and, bracing himself, dipped his hand deep into the foam. A jagger of glass stung him. Gently he removed a broken goblet. The beautiful bowl was intact. He took a fresh dish towel and went on with his household work.

When everything was clean and dry, and the bowl stood aloof and serene on the safest shelf of a cupboard, and the little bright house was securely locked up in the large dark night, Pnin sat down at the kitchen table and, taking a sheet of yellow scrap paper from its drawer, unclipped his fountain pen and started to compose the draft of a letter:

"Dear Hagen," he wrote in his clear firm hand, "permit me to recaputilate (crossed out) recapitulate the conversation we had tonight. It, I must confess, somewhat astonished me. If I had the honor to correctly understand you, you said——"

Chapter Seven

1

My first recollection of Timofey Pnin is connected with a speck of coal dust that entered my left eye on a spring Sunday in 1911.

It was one of those rough, gusty, and lustrous mornings in St. Petersburg, when the last transparent piece of Ladoga ice has been carried away to the gulf by the Neva, and her indigo waves heave and lap the granite of the embankment, and the tugboats and huge barges, moored along the quay, creak and scrape rhythmically, and the mahogany and brass of anchored steam yachts shine in the skittish sun. I had been trying out a beautiful new English bicycle given me for my twelfth birthday, and, as I rode home to our rosy-stone house in the Morskaya, over parquet-smooth wooden pavements, the consciousness of having gravely disobeyed my tutor was less bothersome than the granule of smarting pain in the far north of my eyeball. Home remedies, such as the application of wads of cotton wool soaked in cool tea and the *tri-k-nosu* (rub-noseward) device, only made matters worse; and when I awoke next morning, the object lurking under my upper eyelid felt like a solid polygon that became more deeply embedded at every watery wink. In the afternoon I was taken to a leading ophthalmologist, Dr. Pavel Pnin.

One of those silly incidents that remain forever in a child's receptive mind marked the space of time my tutor and I spent in Dr. Pnin's sundust-and-plush waiting room, where the blue dab of a window in miniature was reflected in the glass dome of an ormolu clock on the mantelpiece, and two flies kept describing slow quadrangles around the lifeless chandelier. A lady, wearing a plumed hat, and her dark-spectacled husband were sitting in connubial silence on the davenport; then a cavalry officer entered and sat near the window reading a newspaper; then the husband repaired to Dr. Pnin's study; and then I noticed an odd expression on my tutor's face.

With my good eye I followed his stare. The officer was leaning toward the lady. In rapid French he berated her for something she had done or not done the day before. She gave him her gloved hand to kiss. He glued himself to its eyelet—and forthwith left, cured of whatever had ailed him.

In softness of features, body bulk, leanness of leg,

apish shape of ear and upper lip, Dr. Pavel Pnin looked very like Timofey, as the latter was to look three or four decades later. In the father, however, a fringe of straw-colored hair relieved a waxlike calvity; he wore a black-rimmed pince-nez on a black ribbon like the late Dr. Chekhov; he spoke in a gentle stutter, very unlike his son's later voice. And what a divine relief it was when, with a tiny instrument resembling an elf's drumstick, the tender doctor removed from my eyeball the offending black atom! I wonder where that speck is now? The dull, mad fact is that it *does* exist somewhere.

Perhaps because on my visits to schoolmates I had seen other middle-class apartments, I unconsciously retained a picture of the Pnin flat that probably corresponds to reality. I can report therefore that as likely as not it consisted of two rows of rooms divided by a long corridor; on one side was the waiting room, the doctor's office, presumably a dining room and a drawing room further on; and on the other side were two or three bedrooms, a schoolroom, a bathroom, a maid's room, and a kitchen. I was about to leave with a phial of eye lotion, and my tutor was taking the opportunity to ask Dr. Pnin if eyestrain might cause gastric trouble, when the front door opened and shut. Dr. Pnin nimbly walked into the passage, voiced a query, received a quiet answer, and returned with his son Timofey, a thirteen-year-old *gimnazist* (classical school pupil) in his *gimnazicheskiy* uniform—black blouse, black pants, shiny black belt (I attended a more liberal school where we wore what we liked).

Do I really remember his crew cut, his puffy pale face, his red ears? Yes, distinctly. I even remember the way he imperceptibly removed his shoulder from under the proud paternal hand, while the proud paternal voice was saying: "This boy has just got a Five Plus (A+) in the Algebra examination." From the end of the corridor there came a steady smell of hashed-cabbage pie, and through the open door of the schoolroom I could see a map of Russia on the wall, books on a shelf, a stuffed squirrel, and a toy monoplane with linen wings and a rubber motor. I had a similar one but twice bigger, bought in Biarritz. After one had wound up the propeller for some time, the rubber would change its manner of twist and develop fascinating thick whorls which predicted the end of its tether.

2

Five years later, after spending the beginning of the summer on our estate near St. Petersburg, my mother, my young brother, and I happened to visit a dreary old aunt at her curiously desolate country seat not far from a famous resort on the Baltic coast. One afternoon, as in concentrated ecstasy I was spreading, underside up, an exceptionally rare aberration of the Paphia Fritillary, in which the silver stripes ornamenting the lower surface of its hindwings had fused into an even expanse of metallic gloss, a footman came up with the information that the old lady requested my presence. In the reception hall I found her talking to two self-conscious youths in university student uniforms. One, with the blond fuzz, was Timofey Pnin, the other, with the russet down, was Grigoriy Belochkin. They had come to ask my grandaunt the permission to use an empty barn on the confines of her property for the staging of a play. This was a Russian translation of Arthur Schnitzler's three-act *Liebelei*. Ancharov, a provincial semiprofessional actor, with a reputation consisting mainly of faded newspaper clippings, was helping to rig up the thing. Would I participate? But at sixteen I was as arrogant as I was shy, and declined to play the anonymous gentleman in Act One. The interview ended in mutual embarrassment, not alleviated by Pnin or Belochkin overturning a glass of pear *kvas,* and I went back to my butterfly. A fortnight later I was somehow or other compelled to attend the performance. The barn was full of *dachniki* (vacationists) and disabled soldiers from a nearby hospital. I came with my brother, and next to me sat the steward of my aunt's estate, Robert Karlovich Horn, a cheerful plump person from Riga with bloodshot, porcelain-blue eyes, who kept applauding heartily at the wrong moments. I remember the odor of decorative fir branches, and the eyes of peasant children glistening through the chinks in the walls. The front seats were so close to the stage that when the betrayed husband produced a packet of love letters written to his wife by Fritz Lobheimer, dragoon and college student, and flung them into Fritz's face, you could see perfectly well that they were old postcards with the stamp corners cut off. I am perfectly sure that the small role of this irate Gentleman was taken by Timofey Pnin (though, of course, he might also have appeared as somebody else in the following acts); but a buff overcoat, bushy mustachios, and a dark wig with a median parting disguised him so thoroughly that the minuscule interest I took in his existence might not have warranted any conscious assurance on my part. Fritz, the young lover doomed to die in a duel, not only has that mysterious affair backstage with the Lady in Black Velvet, the Gentleman's wife, but toys with the heart of Christine, a naïve Viennese maiden. Fritz was played by stocky, forty-year-old Ancharov, who wore a warm-taupe make-up, thumped his chest with the sound of rug beating, and by his impromptu contributions to the role he had not deigned to learn almost paralyzed Fritz's pal, Theodor Kaiser (Grigoriy Belochkin). A moneyed old maid in real life, whom Ancharov humored, was miscast as Christine Weiring, the violinist's daughter. The role of the little milliner, Theodor's amoretta, Mizi Schlager, was charmingly acted by a pretty, slender-necked, velvet-eyed girl, Belochkin's sister, who got the greatest ovation of the night.

3

It is improbable that during the years of Revolution and Civil War which followed I had occasion to recall Dr. Pnin and his son. If I have reconstructed in some detail the precedent impressions, it is merely to fix what flashed through my mind when, on an April night in the early twenties, at a Paris café, I found myself shaking hands with auburn-bearded, infantine-eyed Timofey Pnin, erudite young author of several admirable papers on Russian culture. It was the custom among émigré writers and artists to gather at the Three Fountains after the recitals or lectures that were so popular among Russian expatriates; and it was on such an occasion that, still hoarse from my reading, I tried not only to remind Pnin of former meetings, but also to amuse him and other people around us with the unusual

179

lucidity and strength of my memory. However, he denied everything. He said he vaguely recalled my grandaunt but had never met me. He said that his marks in algebra had always been poor and that, anyway, his father never displayed him to patients; he said that in *Zabava (Liebelei)* he had only acted the part of Christine's father. He repeated that we had never seen each other before. Our little discussion was nothing more than good-natured banter, and everybody laughed; and noticing how reluctant he was to recognize his own past, I switched to another, less personal, topic.

Presently I grew aware that a striking-looking young girl in a black silk sweater, with a golden band around her brown hair, had become my chief listener. She stood before me, right elbow resting on left palm, right hand holding cigarette between finger and thumb as a gypsy would, cigarette sending up its smoke; bright blue eyes half closed because of the smoke. She was Liza Bogolepov, a medical student who also wrote poetry. She asked me if she could send me for appraisal a batch of her poems. A little later at the same party, I noticed her sitting next to a repulsively hairy young composer, Ivan Nagoy; they were drinking *auf Bruderschaft,* which is performed by intertwining arms with one's co-drinker, and some chairs away Dr. Barakan, a talented neurologist and Liza's latest lover, was watching her with quiet despair in his dark almond-shaped eyes.

A few days later she sent me those poems; a fair sample of her production is the kind of stuff that émigré rhymsterettes wrote after Akhmatova: lackadaisical little lyrics that tiptoed in more or less anapaestic tetrameter and sat down rather heavily with a wistful sigh:

> *Samotsvétov króme ochéy*
> *Net u menyá nikakíh,*
> *No est' róza eshchó nezhnéy*
> *Rózovih gúb moíh.*
> *I yúnosha tíhiy skazál:*
> *"Vashe sérdtse vsegó nezhnéy . . ."*
> *I yá opustíla glazá . . .*

I have marked the stress accents, and transliterated the Russian with the usual understanding that *u* is pronounced like a short "oo," *i* like a short "ee," and *zh* like a French "j." Such incomplete rhymes as *skazal-glaza* were considered very elegant. Note also the erotic undercurrents and *cour d'amour* implications. A prose translation would go: "No jewels, save my eyes, do I own, but I have a rose which is even softer than my rosy lips. And a quiet youth said: 'There is nothing softer than your heart.' And I lowered my gaze. . . ."

I wrote back telling Liza that her poems were bad and she ought to stop composing. Sometime later I saw her in another café, sitting at a long table, abloom and ablaze among a dozen young Russian poets. She kept her sapphire glance on me with a mocking and mysterious persistence. We talked. I suggested she let me see those poems again in some quieter place. She did. I told her they struck me as being even worse than they had seemed at the first reading. She lived in the cheapest room of a decadent little hotel with no bath and a pair of twittering young Englishmen for neighbors.

Poor Liza! She had of course her artistic moments

when she would stop, entranced, on a May night in a squalid street to admire—nay, to adore—the motley remains of an old poster on a wet black wall in the light of a street lamp, and the translucent green of linden leaves where they drooped next to the lamp, but she was one of those women who combine healthy good looks with hysterical sloppiness; lyrical outbursts with a very practical and very commonplace mind; a vile temper with sentimentality; and languorous surrender with a robust capacity for sending people on wild-goose errands. In the result of emotions and in the course of events, the narration of which would be of no public interest whatsoever, Liza swallowed a handful of sleeping pills. As she tumbled into unconsciousness she knocked over an open bottle of the deep-red ink which she used to write down her verses, and that bright trickle coming from under her door was noticed by Chris and Lew just in time to have her saved.

I had not seen her for a fortnight after that contretemps when, on the eve of my leaving for Switzerland and Germany, she waylaid me in the little garden at the end of my street, looking svelt and strange in a charming new dress as dove-gray as Paris, and wearing a really enchanting new hat with a blue bird's wing, and handed me a folded paper. "I want a last piece of advice from you," said Liza in what the French call a "white" voice. "This is an offer of marriage that I have received. I shall wait till midnight. If I don't hear from you, I shall accept it." She hailed a taxi and was gone.

The letter has by chance remained among my papers. Here it is:

"I am afraid you will be pained by my confession,

my dear Lise" (the writer, though using Russian, called her throughout by this French form of her name, in order, I presume, to avoid both the too familiar 'Liza' and the too formal 'Elizaveta Innokentievna'). "It is always painful for a sensitive *(chutkiy)* person to see another in an awkward position. And I am definitely in an awkward position.

"You, Lise, are surrounded by poets, scientists, artists, dandies. The celebrated painter who made your portrait last year is now, it is said, drinking himself to death *(govoryat, spilsya)* in the wilds of Massachusetts. Rumor proclaims many other things. And here I am, daring to write to you.

"I am not handsome, I am not interesting, I am not talented. I am not even rich. But, Lise, I offer you everything I have, to the last blood corpuscle, to the last tear, everything. And, believe me, this is more than any genius can offer you because a genius needs to keep so much in store, and thus cannot offer you the whole of himself as I do. I may not achieve happiness, but I know I shall do everything to make you happy. I want you to write poems. I want you to go on with your psychotherapeutic research—in which I do not understand much, while questioning the validity of what I can understand. Incidentally, I am sending you under separate cover a pamphlet published in Prague by my friend Professor Chateau, which brilliantly refutes your Dr. Halp's theory of birth being an act of suicide on the part of the infant. I have permitted myself to correct an obvious misprint on page 48 of Chateau's excellent paper. I await your" (probably "decision," the bottom of the page with the signature had been cut off by Liza).

When half a dozen years later I revisited Paris, I learned that Timofey Pnin had married Liza Bogolepov soon after my departure. She sent me a published collection of her poems *Suhie Gubï* (Dry Lips) with the inscription in dark-red ink: "To a Stranger from a Stranger" *(neznakomtsu ot neznakomki)*. I saw Pnin and her at an evening tea in the apartment of a famous émigré, a social revolutionary, one of those informal gatherings where old-fashioned terrorists, heroic nuns, gifted hedonists, liberals, adventurous young poets, elderly novelists and artists, publishers and publicists, free-minded philosophers and scholars would represent a kind of special knighthood, the active and significant nucleus of an exiled society which during the third of a century it flourished remained practically unknown to American intellectuals, for whom the notion of Russian emigration was made to mean by astute communist propaganda a vague and perfectly fictitious mass of so-called Trotskiites (whatever these are), ruined reactionaries, reformed or disguised Cheka men, titled ladies, professional priests, restaurant keepers, and White Russian military groups, all of them of no cultural importance whatever.

Taking advantage of Pnin's being engaged in a political discussion with Kerenski at the other end of the table, Liza informed me—with her usual crude candor—that she had "told Timofey everything"; that he was "a saint" and had "pardoned" me. Fortunately, she did not often accompany him to later receptions where I had the pleasure of sitting next to him, or opposite him, in the company of dear friends, on our small lone planet, above the black and diamond city, with the lamplight on this or that Socratic cranium and a slice of lemon revolving in the glass of stirred tea. One night, as Dr. Barakan, Pnin, and I were sitting at the Bolotovs, I happened to be talking to the neurologist about a cousin of his, Ludmila, now Lady D——, whom I had known in Yalta, Athens, and London, when suddenly Pnin cried to Dr. Barakan across the table: "Now, don't believe a word he says, Georgiy Aramovich. He makes up everything. He once invented that we were schoolmates in Russia and cribbed at examinations. He is a dreadful inventor *(on uzhasniy vidumshchik)*." Barakan and I were so astounded by this outburst that we just sat and looked at each other in silence.

5

In the rememoration of old relationships, later impressions often tend to be dimmer than earlier ones. I recall talking to Liza and her new husband, Dr. Eric Wind, in between two acts of a Russian play in New York sometime in the early forties. He said he had a "really tender feeling for Herr Professor Pnin" and gave me some bizarre details of their voyage together from Europe in the beginning of World War II. I ran into Pnin several times during those years at various social and academic functions in New York; but the only vivid recollection I have is of our ride together on a west-side bus, on a very festive and very wet night in 1952. We had come from our respective colleges to participate in a literary and artistic program before a large émigré audience in downtown New York on the occasion of the hundredth anniversay of a great writer's death. Pnin had been teaching at Waindell since the mid-forties and never had I seen him look healthier, more prosperous, and more self-assertive. He and I turned out to be, as he quipped, *vos'midesyatniki* (men of the Eighties), that is, we both happened to have lodgings for the night in the West Eighties; and as we hung from adjacent straps in the crowded and spasmodic vehicle, my good friend managed to combine a vigorous ducking and twisting of the head (in his continuous attempts to check and recheck the numbers of cross streets) with a magnificent account of all he had not had sufficient time to say at the celebration on Homer's and Gogol's use of the Rambling Comparison.

6

When I decided to accept a professorship at Waindell, I stipulated that I could invite whomever I wanted for teaching in the special Russian Division I planned to inaugurate. With this confirmed, I wrote to Timofey Pnin offering him in the most cordial terms I could muster to assist me in any way and to any extent he desired. His answer surprised me and hurt me. Curtly he wrote that he was through with teaching and would not even bother to wait till the end of the spring term. Then he turned to other subjects. Victor (about whom I had politely inquired) was in Rome with his mother; she had divorced her third husband and married an Italian art dealer. Pnin concluded his letter by saying that to his great regret he would be leaving Waindell two or three days before the public lecture that I was to give there Tuesday, February the fifteenth. He did not specify his destination.

The Greyhound that brought me to Waindell on Monday the fourteenth arrived after nightfall. I was met by the Cockerells, who treated me to a late supper at their house, where I discovered I was to spend the night, instead of sleeping at a hotel as I had hoped. Gwen Cockerell turned out to be a very pretty woman in her late thirties, with a kitten's profile and graceful limbs. Her husband, whom I had once met in New Haven and remembered as a rather limp, moon-faced, neutrally blond Englishman, had acquired an unmistakable resemblance to the man he had now been mimicking for almost ten years. I was tired and not overanxious to be entertained throughout the supper with a floor show, but I must admit that Jack Cockerell impersonated Pnin to perfection. He went on for at least two hours, showing me everything—Pnin teaching, Pnin eating, Pnin ogling a coed, Pnin narrating the epic of the electric fan which he had imprudently set going on a glass shelf right above the bathtub into which its own vibration had almost caused it to fall; Pnin trying to convince Professor Wynn, the ornithologist who hardly knew him, that they were old pals, Tim and Tom—and Wynn leaping to the conclusion that this was somebody impersonating Professor Pnin. It was all built of course around the Pninian gesture and the Pninian wild English, but Cockerell also managed to imitate such things as the subtle degree of difference between the silence of Pnin and the silence of Thayer, as they sat motionlessly ruminating in adjacent chairs at the Faculty Club. We got Pnin in the Stacks, and Pnin on the Campus Lake. We heard Pnin criticize the various rooms he had successively rented. We listened to Pnin's account of his learning to drive a car, and of his dealing with his first puncture on the way back from "the chicken farm of some Privy Counselor of the Tsar," where Cockerell supposed Pnin spent the summers. We arrived at last to Pnin's declaration one day that he had been "shot" by which, according to the impersonator, the poor fellow meant "fired"—(a mistake I doubt my friend could have made). Brilliant Cockerell also told of the strange feud between Pnin and his compatriot Komarov—the mediocre muralist who had kept adding fresco portraits of faculty members in the college dining hall to those already depicted there by the great Lang. Although Komarov belonged to another political faction than Pnin, the patriotic artist had seen in Pnin's dismissal an anti-Russian gesture and had started to delete a sulky Napoleon that stood between young, plumpish (now gaunt) Blorenge and young, mustached (now shaven) Hagen, in order to paint in Pnin; and there was the scene between Pnin and President Poore at lunch—an enraged, spluttering Pnin losing all control over what English he had, pointing a shaking forefinger at the preliminary outlines of a ghostly muzhik on the wall, and shouting that he would sue the college if his face appeared above that blouse; and there was his audience, imperturbable Poore, trapped in the dark of his total blindness, waiting for Pnin to peter out and then asking at large: "Is that foreign gentleman on our staff?" Oh, the impersonation was deliciously funny, and although Gwen Cockerell must have heard the program many times before, she laughed so loud that their old dog Sobakevich, a brown cocker with a tearstained face, began to fidget and sniff at me. The performance, I repeat, was magnificent, but it was too long. By midnight the fun began to thin; the smile I was keeping afloat began to develop, I felt, symptoms of labial cramp. Finally the whole thing grew to be such a bore that I fell wondering if by some poetical vengeance this Pnin business had not become with Cockerell the kind of fatal obsession which substitutes its own victim for that of the initial ridicule.

We had been having a good deal of Scotch, and sometime after midnight Cockerell made one of those sudden decisions that seem so bright and gay at a certain stage of intoxication. He said he was sure foxy old Pnin had not really left yesterday, but was lying low. So why not telephone and find out? He made the call, and although there was no answer to the series of compelling notes which simulate the far sound of actual ringing in an imaginary hallway, it stood to reason that this perfectly healthy telephone would have been probably disconnected, had Pnin really vacated the house. I was foolishly eager to say something friendly to my good Timofey Pahlich, and so after a little while I attempted to reach him too. Suddenly there was a click, a sonic vista, the response of a heavy breathing, and then a poorly disguised voice said: "He is not at home, he has gone, he has quite gone"—after which the speaker hung up; but none save my old friend, not even his best imitator, could rhyme so emphatically "at" with the German "*hat*," "home" with the French "*homme*," and "gone" with the head of "Goneril." Cockerell then proposed driving over to 999 Todd Road and serenading its burrowed tenant, but here Mrs. Cockerell intervened; and after an evening that somehow left me with the mental counterpart of a bad taste in the mouth, we all went to bed.

I spent a poor night in a charming, airy, prettily furnished room where neither window nor door closed
properly, and where an omnibus edition of Sherlock
Holmes which had pursued me for years supported a
bedside lamp, so weak and wan that the set of galleys
I had brought with me to correct could not sweeten
insomnia. The thunder of trucks rocked the house
every two minutes or so; I kept dozing off and sitting
up with a gasp, and through the parody of a window
shade some light from the street reached the mirror and
dazzled me into thinking I was facing a firing squad.

I am so constituted that I absolutely must gulp down
the juice of three oranges before confronting the rigors
of day. So at seven-thirty I took a quick shower, and
five minutes later was out of the house in the company
of the long-eared and dejected Sobakevich.

The air was keen, the sky clear and burnished.
Southward the empty road could be seen ascending a
gray-blue hill among patches of snow. A tall leafless
poplar, as brown as a broom, rose on my right, and
its long morning shadow crossing to the opposite side
of the street reached there a crenulated, cream-colored
house which, according to Cockerell, had been thought
by my predecessor to be the Turkish Consulate on
account of crowds of fez wearers he had seen entering.
I turned left, northward, and walked a couple of blocks
downhill to a restaurant that I had noted on the eve;
but the place had not opened yet, and I turned back.
Hardly had I taken a couple of steps when a great
truck carrying beer rumbled up the street, immediately
followed by a small pale blue sedan with the white

head of a dog looking out, after which came another great truck, exactly similar to the first. The humble sedan was crammed with bundles and suitcases; its driver was Pnin. I emitted a roar of greeting, but he did not see me, and my only hope was that I might walk uphill fast enough to catch him while the red light one block ahead kept him at bay.

I hurried past the rear truck, and had another glimpse of my old friend, in tense profile, wearing a cap with ear flaps and a storm coat; but next moment the light turned green, the little white dog leaning out yapped at Sobakevich, and everything surged forward—truck one, Pnin, truck two. From where I stood I watched them recede in the frame of the roadway, between the Moorish house and the Lombardy poplar. Then the little sedan boldly swung past the front truck and, free at last, spurted up the shining road, which one could make out narrowing to a thread of gold in the soft mist where hill after hill made beauty of distance, and where there was simply no saying what miracle might happen.

Cockerell, brown-robed and sandaled, let in the cocker and led me kitchenward, to a British breakfast of depressing kidney and fish.

"And now," he said, "I am going to tell you the story of Pnin rising to address the Cremona Women's Club and discovering he had brought the wrong lecture."